SUMMER DAYS ON SUNFLOWER STREET

A SWEET, FEEL-GOOD ROMANCE TO WARM YOUR HEART

SUNFLOWER STREET
BOOK 2

RACHEL GRIFFITHS

COSY COTTAGE BOOKS

Copyright © 2020 by RACHEL GRIFFITHS
All rights reserved.
No part of this book may be reproduced in any form or by any electronic or mechanical means, including information storage and retrieval systems, without written permission from the author, except for the use of brief quotations in a book review.

❀ Created with Vellum

For my family, with love always.
XXXX

SUMMER DAYS ON SUNFLOWER STREET

Roxie Walker has been married to **Fletcher** for over twenty years. They live in a beautiful house on **Sunflower Street**, have a cute pug named Glenda and enjoy a comfortable lifestyle. However, Roxie has a feeling that something isn't quite right…

Fletcher works hard and likes to relax on his days off, whether that's playing a round of golf, watching a football match on TV, or pottering around in the garden. Recently, though, he's finding it hard to switch off and he's concerned that Roxie seems to be drifting away from him. He comes up with a plan to try to make things better, but the secrecy required to carry it out creates its own problems.

As summer descends upon Sunflower Street, with warmer days spent at the recently refurbished lido and lighter evenings enjoyed in their lovely garden, matters come to a head. It's time for the truth to be revealed, and for grievances – both old and new – to be aired.

Will summer on Sunflower Street bring Roxie and Fletcher closer together or will it tear them apart?

1

'Right, Glenda, you wait there… I won't be a moment,' Roxie Walker pointed at the paved area outside the rear of her house. The small fawn pug gazed up at her, bulbous brown eyes unblinking. 'I just need to get something from the shed.'

Glenda licked her lips as if demonstrating her understanding, then peered up at the clear blue sky. Roxie looked up too, watching as two birds soared high above, circling the house and fields beyond. Probably red kites or kestrels.

The soft grass of her lawn was springy underfoot as Roxie crossed it to reach the far end of the back garden, then climbed the three wide stone steps that led to the raised decking. Her flip-flops slapped against her heels as she moved across the decking before opening the shed door.

The aromas of warm wood and compost greeted her, and she breathed them in, savouring the scents of summer. It had been a sunny June day and the interior of the shed was almost tropical. She scanned the shelves until she spotted her gardening gloves and secateurs, picked them up, then turned and went back outside.

Once she'd descended to the grass again, Roxie headed over to the rambling rose bushes that had been planted all those years ago in front of the high wooden fence. She breathed in their heady aroma, her heartbeat quickening, her fingers itching to caress the soft petals, soft as a baby's skin. With warmer weather over the past fortnight, the rose bushes had filled out and she wanted to tidy them up a bit and to take a few of the flowers to press.

Glenda appeared as she worked, clearly forgetting Roxie's instruction to remain on the patio – or at least believing it only applied while Roxie went to the shed, which it did because Glenda had a thing about capturing any spiders she saw in the shed and taking them back to the house – then sat on the grass by her feet, watching her carefully. Roxie dropped leaves and twigs into a green waste bag and flowers into the basket she'd brought outside earlier. Now that the flowers had been disturbed, the air was heavy with their potent aroma, stirring Roxie's emotions.

'Aren't they pretty, Glenda?' Roxie asked, and the dog gave a small bark. 'One pink and one white. I wanted a baby, but I got two rose bushes.'

Roxie gave a wan smile then peered around as if worried someone might have overheard her. But there was no chance of that because the garden was so private and because she knew she'd spoken softly. It was something she did whenever she allowed these thoughts to enter her mind, as if she was keeping her voice soft and low for the babies she'd never had, not wanting to upset them with her own pain.

She snipped the stem of a pink rose and held it to her face, inhaling its sweetness, feeling the soft caress of the petals against her skin. Would a baby's skin have been this silky? This pure and perfect? She dropped the rose into the basket then cut a few more until she had an equal mix of pink and white flowers.

'That will do for now, Glenda.'

The dog gave a small growl and raced off towards the house, ran inside, then reemerged and returned to Roxie with her squidgy blue ball. She dropped it at Roxie's feet then stood right in front of her, tensed and ready to spring.

'What's that, Glenda? You want me to throw this for you?'

The pug turned in circles, her breaths rasping, her tongue lolling from her open mouth.

'Really?'

Glenda barked, so Roxie bowled the ball across the grass and laughed as Glenda pursued it, her small legs moving so quickly she almost did a forward roll.

They repeated the process five times then Roxie picked up the basket of flowers and hooked the handle over her arm, grabbed the green bag of garden waste and walked towards the house. Glenda trotted beside her, the ball between her jaws, her curly little tail held high.

'Thank goodness for dogs, eh, Glenda?' Roxie smiled down at the pug, her tiny but sturdy canine companion. 'I don't know what I'd do without you.'

As Roxie entered the kitchen, the doorbell rang, echoing through the house. Simultaneously, her mobile buzzed in the pocket of her cropped jeans and she pulled it out to see an alert from the video doorbell.

'Oh look, it's Ethan come to get on with his work.' She showed the screen to Glenda and the dog tilted her head. She spoke into the phone, 'Won't be a moment.'

She set the basket down on the dresser in the hallway then went to open the door.

'Hello, Ethan.'

As he stepped inside, he sniffed the air.

'Smells like roses in here, Roxie.'

Roxie smiled and gestured at the basket. 'You're welcome to take some for Lila if you want.'

'That'd be great, thanks.' He nodded. 'Right, I'd better get back to work.'

'And I'll pop the kettle on.'

Roxie returned to the kitchen and went about making tea, humming as she worked, glad to have some human company around, even if it was just the decorator.

~

Fletcher looked up from his smartphone and his gaze fell on the elderly man sitting opposite. The man had fallen asleep, his jaw slack, no doubt rocked into slumber by the gentle jogging motion of the train that ran from Waterloo to Wisteria Hollow and beyond. It was only Monday, but Fletcher felt like he could close his eyes and fall asleep too. It had been a very busy day.

It wasn't a bad commute, just thirty minutes to the Surrey village, but the trains were often busy, especially at peak times. Fletcher would avoid those times if he could, but waiting for later trains meant getting home later, and he often preferred to stand for the journey rather than not reach home until gone seven p.m. Of course, some days he couldn't avoid that because of meetings and client dinners, but as often as possible, he came home as soon as he could, even though he had a feeling Roxie suspected he didn't make this his priority.

Turning his gaze to the window, he watched as houses, industrial estates and fields flew past in a blur like some kind of smudged watercolour. A lot of the time he barely noticed what the train passed because he was either checking his emails on his phone, thinking about work or occasionally on a late business call.

He wondered how Ethan had got on today with the painting. Roxie had hired her friend Lila's boyfriend to paint their house, claiming that it needed freshening up. Fletcher wasn't sure that it did, aware that it had only been done about a year ago, but Roxie had insisted, and Fletcher wasn't going to argue with her. After all, she spent far more time at home than he did, and she liked keeping the house looking nice. In fact, Fletcher really appreciated her efforts. The only thing about it that bothered him was when he started to worry that it was Roxie's way of avoiding thinking about other things. She filled her days with exercise, meeting friends, organising village events, cooking, cleaning, gardening, and updating the interior design of their home and furnishings. Fletcher liked being busy too, as time to think could be time to dwell on things he'd prefer to forget, but Roxie was often like a whirlwind, twisting and turning in a way that made him dizzy.

His wife was an incredible woman. She'd always amazed him with her quiet determination, her caring nature and her ability to see the positives in most situations. From the first moment he'd seen her, Fletcher had known that she was the woman he wanted to spend his life with. The early days of their relationship had been passionate, intense and overwhelming, and he had been consumed by his feelings for her. Even now, remembering those feelings made his stomach flutter. But time and life had chipped away at them both and he knew that he wasn't as attentive as he could be these days, that he wasn't always the husband Roxie needed, but he did try. He really did. Yet long days at work as a senior buyer for a supermarket chain, with so much responsibility on his shoulders, combined with the daily grind of being human, exhausted him. Sometimes, he just didn't have the energy to apply to his marriage that he'd had in the early days. It wasn't a lack of love, desire or appreciation that stopped him being what he wanted to be for Roxie, it was just that he was older and far more tired than he used to be.

He had wanted to be a good husband and provider. Roxie would have gone out to work, he knew that, but he hadn't wanted her to *have* to work. He had an image of himself as being there for her, taking care of her and giving her everything she wanted. It was a lot of pressure to put on himself, especially when he worried he was getting it wrong on more than one level, but it had worked over the years. Had he been able to don a cape and wear his underpants over his trousers, Fletcher would have been the superhero he had wanted to be as a child and wooed his wife every day. But in real life, heroes didn't wear costumes, they were ordinary unassuming folks who did their best. He was trying to do his best.

Summer Days on Sunflower Street

As the train slowed, the brakes screeched, the sound grating through him and making him shudder. The old man opposite jolted awake, smacking his lips together before wiping at his chin with the back of a gnarled hand. He caught Fletcher watching him and raised his eyebrows, nodded then offered an apologetic smile. Fletcher smiled back.

'Long day?' Fletcher asked.

'Very long day,' the man replied. 'I've been to the funeral of a school chum's wife. Very sad affair. Lovely woman she was. Taken too soon.'

'Sorry to hear that.' Fletcher gave an understanding nod. 'How old was she?'

'Seventy-eight. Known them both since school and gosh she was a beauty, inside and out. Her husband will be lost without her. In fact… I don't know how he'll manage.' His eyes glistened and he lowered his gaze to the table before clearing his throat several times.

'Seventy-eight is young these days.' Fletcher swallowed hard, the tightening in his own throat surprising him. He wasn't usually this caught up in someone else's grief. He must be getting soft.

'Aye, it is indeed.' The old man met his eyes again. 'I'll turn eighty next week and I still feel the same as I did at eighteen. A bit more weathered, a bit creakier…' He held up his hands and stared at them as if surprised by their swollen joints, brown spots and the veins that protruded from his thin skin. 'But time somehow gets away from you and before you know it, your life is behind you.'

Fletcher's throat constricted even more, and he gave a small cough as if to dislodge the uncomfortable feeling. 'I... uh...' What could he say to reassure the man who quite clearly could do with some words of wisdom? Did he even have any suitable platitudes that wouldn't sound clichéd and weak?

'It's all right, son.' The man smiled. 'Don't mind me. Denise lived a good life, gave birth to five beautiful daughters and made Bill very happy. At the end of the day, it's all we can do. Make the most of every moment, won't you?'

Fletcher nodded, unable to reply, but he took the man's message and held it in his heart. He had always tried to make the most of every day, but it didn't hurt to have a reminder now and then, to refocus on the present. When he got home, he was going to give his wife the biggest hug she'd had in years.

The train came to a halt in line with the platform and the man stood up, straightened his tie then stepped into the aisle. He flashed Fletcher a smile, pushed his shoulders back then made his way to the end of the carriage, leaving Fletcher impatient to reach his own stop.

2

'Are you sure about this?' Lila asked Roxie as they stood in front of the beauty salon that Friday afternoon.

'Of course, I'm sure, Lila.' Roxie smiled at her friend. 'Why?'

'Well… it's not really me, is it?'

'What isn't?'

'All this glamour stuff.'

Roxie giggled. 'Lila, we're not about to have cosmetic surgery you know, there will be no nips or tucks today.'

'No, I know. But… I like having my hair done and sometimes my nails but as for other stuff… well…'

'Don't be silly, Lila, this will do us both good. Besides which, The Beauty Lounge is new to the village and it will be a good thing if we support it with our patronage.'

Lila wrinkled her nose and stared at the front of the salon. Roxie followed her gaze, taking in the shopfront with its shiny windows and bright pink woodwork. There were photos of models with the latest hairstyles and with impossibly long eyelashes, then there were some of men with completely hairless chests and one of a naked couple walking away from the camera along a tropical beach as the sun set. Okay, so the photographs might be a bit daunting – and possibly irrelevant in the case of the naked couple – but no one looked that way without effort. Besides which, she thought it would do her and Lila good to have a few hours of pampering.

'Come on, Lila, we're booked in for two p.m. and it's a minute past now.'

'I'm nervous.' Lila's blue eyes widened, and Roxie took her hand.

'It will be fun. Trust me.'

As Roxie pushed open the door and they stepped inside, she hoped that her friend would discover that she was right.

~

Fletcher was sitting in his office gazing out at the wonderful view. The various landmarks of commercial London stood tall and proud; the windows of The Gherkin, The Cheesegrater, The Scalpel and The Shard all sparkling in the afternoon sunshine. His office in the City building was evidence of his position in the company, a reward for all the years of hard graft and loyalty that he'd put in. It was spacious, bright and airy – everything, from the walls to the doors, was made of glass so that the whole of the floor had an air of transparency and openness, of equality and shared goals. It was what he'd dreamt of as a young man, what many of his junior colleagues probably dreamt of and one day – though he didn't really care to dwell on it right now – his job and office would belong to someone else and Fletcher would be like the old man he'd met on the train the other day. If he was lucky enough to live to eighty, that was.

A tapping on the door made him turn on his swivel chair. He nodded at the young woman standing behind the glass and she pushed the door open, smiling as she strode in on impossibly high heels that coordinated with her fitted red dress.

'Cynthia.' He took a deep breath, wondering what his colleague wanted, preparing himself for whatever initiative she'd come up with now. Cynthia was one of his team and very ambitious, so much so that she was known for being quite blunt – bordering on verbally brutal – with those around her, because, as she had told Fletcher, she didn't 'suffer fools gladly'.

Fletcher admired her single-mindedness; she was highly competent and knew exactly what she wanted, and how she intended on getting there. She'd told him on more than one occasion that she aspired to have his job and then to climb even higher. He had wished her luck and she had inclined her head graciously, what could have been viewed as a vulpine smile playing on her red lips. He had tried to ignore the way she'd rested her hand on his arm over after-work drinks on several occasions and held his gaze until he'd been forced to look away, how she'd leant in close as she'd asked him if he'd like another Martini and how her heavy perfume had lingered on his suit jacket all the way home on the train. It was as if everything was a power play for Cynthia and she was hungry to prove herself in more ways than one, as if she needed to know that she was as beautiful as she was intelligent. With her flawless skin, piercing blue eyes and shiny curtain of blonde hair, Cynthia was certainly attractive. Fletcher wasn't blind, he could see that and other colleagues evidently did too. But Fletcher knew that it was her intelligence, her drive and ambition, along with people skills (and she needed to work on these) that would help her achieve what she wanted career wise, and nothing related to her appearance.

In some ways, Cynthia even reminded him a bit of how Roxie had been during the early days of their courtship, of how she'd sparkled with confidence and ambition, with an exuberant joy in life and an eagerness to get everything she could out of it.

Fletcher had loved Roxie back then, and he loved her now.

As much as always?

Yes ... of course.

'I was just wondering if you wanted to grab some lunch, Fletcher?' Cynthia had come around to the side of his desk and she was so close he could have touched her hand if he'd reached out. Her perfume filled his office, strong and cloying, and he tried not to breathe it in. She didn't wait for an answer but instead stepped closer to the window and gazed out at the view, lifting one foot slightly, probably to ease the throbbing in her toes, Fletcher thought, looking at the sharply pointed stiletto heels. 'What do you think?' she asked without turning around.

At that moment, Fletcher's stomach grumbled, and he realised that he was actually hungry.

'Sounds like a good idea.' He stood up. 'Eating in or out?'

Cynthia turned then and he felt the full force of her steely blue gaze.

'Out, of course, Fletcher. It is Friday after all.'

~

'Mmmm ... That's so good.'

Roxie peered at Lila who was lying face down on the massage table.

'Oh... yes...'

Roxie sniggered. 'Told you that you'd enjoy it.'

Lila lifted her head. Her blonde hair was messy, her cheeks flushed, and her eyes dreamy. She looked almost drunk.

'It's *so* good. Why have I never had a professional massage before?'

Roxie shrugged. 'Never too late to start.'

'Oh, believe me, I'll be booking many more of these.' Lila closed her eyes and dropped her head again. The masseuse flashed a smile at Roxie then continued her firm manipulation of Lila's back.

Roxie lowered her head and allowed the delicious sensations to flow through her as she enjoyed her own massage. She'd booked herself and Lila in for a massage, manicure and pedicure, and finally, for waxing. Knowing that Lila would be apprehensive, she'd booked the massage first to relax her and the waxing last because she knew it would be likely to make Lila run for the hills if it was the first treatment of the day.

Closing her eyes, she breathed deeply, allowing her mind to wander. She knew she was lucky being able to come to the salon on a Friday afternoon when many people would be at work. She'd left Ethan decorating her dining room, telling Glenda to behave as the small pug sat watching him from the doorway. Glenda had taken to Ethan as she did to most men and Ethan seemed to like her just as much, fussing over Glenda when he arrived and before he left in the evenings. He'd even brought Glenda some treats and a toy, so Roxie knew that Glenda would be his friend for life.

And, of course, her mind drifted, as it always did, to Fletcher. Deep in the heart of London, what would he be doing right now? Reading emails? Scanning a document? Sitting in a meeting? Or would he be eating lunch, possibly with a client or colleague, his suit jacket open, his tie loosened at the neck exposing his throat and that triangle of skin where Roxie loved to plant soft kisses, where she could smell his woody cologne and the delicious scent of his skin that was his and his alone.

She stretched out and released a sigh. She was so lucky to have such a good husband and to be as deeply in love with him as she had been when they'd married. More in fact. Some couples lost touch, their connection faded, and they forgot about why they'd fallen in love in the first place. Roxie never had. All the old passion she'd felt for Fletcher was still there, although it was quieter now because she kept it that way, simmering beneath the surface so as not to overwhelm her quiet, serious, hardworking husband. It was, she thought, almost as if she was afraid of startling him with how much she cared, as if she felt she was too much for him and would scare him away if she let him know exactly how much she adored him still.

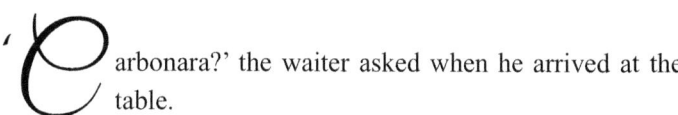

'Carbonara?' the waiter asked when he arrived at the table.

'That's me.' Fletcher held up a hand and the waiter set the large pasta bowl down in front of him. 'Thank you.'

While the rest of the table received their orders, Fletcher stared at the steaming bowl of pasta in front of him. It looked creamy, rich and delicious, but he knew he shouldn't really eat it. He ran a hand over stomach, smoothing the curve of his belly under his Ralph Lauren shirt. He was getting a bit of a paunch and needed to reduce his calorie intake, but with work lunches, drinks, and Roxie's wonderful culinary skills, plus the fact that he was getting older and his metabolism slowing down, his waistline was steadily increasing. Unlike Roxie's, because she was as gorgeous as the day they met. Her body was softer, yes, in some ways; her breasts fuller, her hips and bottom gently curved, but she looked good. Fletcher wondered, not for the first time, if she ever looked at him and wished he'd make more of an effort to stay in shape. He hated the thought of her eyeing him when he got out of the shower and seeing a body she no longer found attractive instead of the man she'd fallen for all those years ago. He would do something about it soon for sure. He'd seen Ethan running around the village, so perhaps he'd ask the younger man to train him, or even have a few sessions with that personal trainer Roxie raved about. Yes. That's what he'd do… as soon as he had a bit more time.

'Everything all right?' Cynthia asked from his side, nodding at his bowl.

'Yes! It's perfect.'

'You haven't touched it yet, Fletcher.' She pursed her lips, knitting her brows together.

'About to get stuck in…' Fletcher held up his fork.

'Let's have some wine, shall we? It is almost the weekend.'

Cynthia held up a hand, waving her long slender fingers, and a waiter hurried over. Before Fletcher had even tasted his pasta, he had a large glass of ice-cold white wine next to his bowl and Cynthia was raising her glass for a toast.

Each of his colleagues – there were twelve of them in total, as Cynthia had asked around their floor, encouraging them to attend a team lunch – made a brief toast then it was Fletcher's turn.

He raised his glass, noticing how the condensation on the outside made the wine appear cloudy, the glass slippery in his hand.

'To a … uh … a great weekend!'

His colleagues echoed his toast, glasses were clinked together, wine sipped and swallowed. It was good wine, and Fletcher drank it down in three gulps. He felt it making its way through his empty belly, filtering quickly into his bloodstream.

'Have some more.' Cynthia refilled his glass then her own and he saw no point in resisting.

The next half an hour passed in a blur of wine and pasta, and Fletcher realised that he was likely to want a nap more than an afternoon of work at this rate. It wasn't like him to drink much over lunch, but something about the week had left him wanting some comfort, to feel the gentle buzz of a few glasses of wine and the numbing effect it put between his mind and the outside world. The old man he'd spoken to five days ago on the train had made an impression on him and he'd found it hard to forget the message about making the most of the time he was given. Fletcher felt as though something big was on the horizon, as if something was going to happen and he wouldn't be able to control it whatever he said or did. Of course, he wasn't far away from his fiftieth birthday and it could well have been that, the pressure of entering his next decade looming ahead like a dark tunnel filled with the unknown, and if so, then that was understandable. Anyone would feel some trepidation as they reached the next milestone in their life, wouldn't they? Forty had been a big one for him but even more so for Roxie. It had been as though when she reached forty, Roxie believed her fertile days were well and truly over and she'd finally closed the door on the prospect of children. Fletcher had closed that door long before he turned forty, but for different reasons. Reasons he had buried deeply and hoped never to have to face up to ever again.

'Come on, Fletcher, cheer up!' It was Cynthia again, turning back to him after chatting to other colleagues. 'It can't be *that* bad now can it?'

'I'm fine, honestly.' Fletcher bobbed his head. 'Just a bit tired. It's been a busy week.'

'Poor darling, you're getting old.' Cynthia giggled then placed a cool hand over his and his fork clanked against the bowl. 'But you still remind me of Harrison Ford at his best.'

She beamed at him, exposing pearly white teeth between shiny red lips. Her eyes appraised him, her hand stayed where it was, and Fletcher's stomach lurched. What exactly was going on here? He'd interacted with thousands of female colleagues and clients over the years, but the relationships had only ever been professional. He'd seen his fair share of colleagues get involved, have affairs, betray their partners and spouses, but never done it himself. He'd been far too in love with Roxie to so much as *notice* another woman, but Cynthia? She dressed well, wore extremely expensive (if cloying) perfume and walked into every room as if she owned it.

She was… gorgeous.

Confusing.

Sometimes intimidating.

And now, she was gently stroking Fletcher's hand with her little finger, a movement so small as not to be noticed by the others sitting at their table, but for Fletcher it was soothing, hypnotic and magnifying the effects of the wine.

He opened his mouth to speak but nothing came out.

He thought of Roxie, of Glenda, their home and the life they shared.

Then he met Cynthia's eyes and he knew what he had to do. It was inevitable, inescapable and he knew now that it had been on the cards for some time.

'Cynthia…' He swallowed hard. 'There's something I need to speak to you about. You see… I only have eyes for one woman.'

'I know.' She nodded. 'Let's get out of here.'

As she stood up and smoothed down her dress, Fletcher placed his fork on the table and sighed. He was at a crossroads, but as far as he could see, there was only one direction to take.

3

Roxie and Lila had been massaged and exfoliated, had their fingernails and toenails painted, and now they were waiting outside the waxing rooms. Roxie was incredibly relaxed and she could easily have slid down the sofa they were sitting on and snoozed the afternoon away.

The salon was a converted house on the main street in Wisteria Hollow. The ground floor had been converted into a hair salon, the cellar into a mini spa – complete with massage rooms and Jacuzzi – and the upper floor into beauty treatment rooms. Lila seemed more relaxed than Roxie had ever seen her look before, with her blonde hair swept back with a wide white towelling headband, dreamy eyes and rosy cheeks.

Since Roxie had helped Lila clear out her cottage and donate her wedding dress and accessories to the greyhound charity shop, Lila had been looking better anyway, especially with the arrival of Ethan Morris in the village. He'd had a very positive effect upon Lila, which Roxie was incredibly relieved about, because when Lila had been jilted by her former fiancé (Ben the bastard, as Roxie thought of him) she had been broken-hearted. Roxie had worried that Lila would never let another man into her heart, but gradually, widower Ethan was helping Lila to trust again. Roxie knew that it wasn't easy for Ethan either, and Lila had told her that Ethan had confessed to being afraid of falling in love with Lila then losing her too. The poor man had lost his wife to breast cancer, which was why he'd returned to Sunflower Street to stay with his mother, Freda. He was fragile and vulnerable, but whenever Roxie saw him with Lila, it was obvious that they cared about each other and Roxie hoped with all her heart that it would work out between them. Lila deserved to be happy and Roxie believed that Ethan could make her happy if they were able to surrender to their feelings and let go of old fears.

'Is this going to hurt a lot?' Lila asked as she chewed at a fingernail. Roxie slapped the hand away from Lila's mouth.

'Don't do that! You'll ruin the manicure.'

Lila's eyes widened. 'Oops! I'm nervous and I forgot about the gel polish.' She held out her hand and inspected the nails. 'Will it?'

'Will what?' Roxie frowned.

'Will the waxing hurt?'

'Haven't you ever had anything waxed before?'

'No. I've always shaved or used depilatory cream. I'm a bit of a baby when it comes to pain and I just couldn't seem to summon the courage to be waxed.'

'You pluck your eyebrows though?' Roxie ran a finger over one of Lila's neat brows.

'Yes, but only the stray ones underneath. It stings, so I don't go mad.'

'You have lovely natural brows anyway, Lila, so leave them alone or you'll have to shade them in like I do.'

Lila peered at Roxie's brows. 'I didn't realise.'

Roxie laughed. 'I've been doing it so long that it looks natural now. You should see me first thing in the morning, though. I look permanently surprised.'

Lila giggled. 'I can't imagine you without brows.'

'Oh, I have brows but they're very thin. It was fashionable when I was a teenager to have fine brows, so I plucked all the hairs away, then when I wanted thicker brows, they never grew back properly.'

'Yikes.' Lila's hands flew to her eyebrows.

'Exactly. So, leave yours alone.'

'This *is* going to hurt isn't it?' Lila raised her legs and Roxie looked down at them.

'Good grief, Lila! For a fair-haired person, your leg hair is quite… thick and dark.'

Lila sniggered. 'I know. It always has been. I would have shaved but you told me to let them grow out. Besides which, who sees them?'

'Ethan?' Roxie asked and Lila's cheeks turned from pink to red.

'Not really. Not yet. It's still early days.'

Roxie nodded. 'Of course, it is, honey, and you wait until you're ready before you... before... you do you know what.'

'You know what?' Lila waggled her eyebrows.

'You know what I mean.'

'I do.' Lila stared at her legs as if they had the answers to every question she'd ever wanted to ask, a smile playing on her lips.

'Not to pry...' Roxie placed a hand on Lila's arm. 'But are you having your bikini line done too?'

Lila's eyes widened as she met Roxie's gaze.

'Does that hurt?'

'It stings a bit the first few times, but it gets easier with time.'

'Ooh. I don't know.'

'Think about when we go to the lido.'

Lila nodded. 'I do want to go swimming.'

'Then you best have the bikini line done. Just don't ask for a Brazilian or anything too dramatic and you'll be fine.'

'A Brazilian?'

'Lila, you are so innocent sometimes.'

After she'd explained about the different types of waxing available and Lila had decided to remain as conservative as possible, the door to one of the beauty rooms opened and a woman in a white tunic top and black trousers stepped out.

'Okay, who's going first?'

'Lila.' Roxie nudged Lila's arm.

'Am I? Can't I go second?'

'Probably best if you go first, honey. Get it over and done with.'

Roxie wasn't going to admit it, but she worried that if she went in first, Lila would lose her nerve and scarper.

'Okay then…' Lila stood up and lifted her chin in a gesture of bravery, but the fact that she simultaneously folded her arms across her chest told Roxie that Lila was very nervous indeed.

'You've got this, Lila.' She gave her friend a double thumbs up.

'Yes, I have.' Lila grimaced.

And as she disappeared into the room and the door closed behind her, Roxie couldn't help worrying that Lila was going to hate her for making her go through with this.

∼

Outside the restaurant, Fletcher pushed his hands back through his hair. There was a sense of inevitability about this whole situation and now that it was actually happening, it was obvious that it would have come to this sooner or later. Some things in life were just too difficult to avoid, too exhausting to fight, and however hard a person tried, they would happen, come what may.

This was one of those times.

Cynthia peered up at him, her eyes dark with something that could be desire and her cheeks flushed, though he suspected the flush was to do with the amount of wine she'd drunk.

'Fletcher,' she said breathily, and he winced at the potency of the alcohol on her breath. 'Where shall we go? Back to mine?'

He braced himself. It was now or never.

'Cynthia... I agree that we should go.'

She placed a hand on his tie and leant in towards him. 'Yes, we should. Absolutely. That's what I meant.'

He rubbed the back of his neck. 'Look... Cynthia, I'm not quite sure what you think is going on here... or what you think is going to happen, but I don't think you want it as much as you think you do.'

Her eyes bulged. 'What?'

'Look... uh...' He didn't want to offend her or patronise her, but he didn't know how else to phrase his thoughts. 'I think you've had too much to drink.'

'You've been drinking too.'

'Not much, or not as much as you at any rate. I probably should have stopped you refilling my glass, but I was a bit distracted.'

'Oh, come on, Fletcher. This has been on the cards for months. Years, even!' She flung her hand back and the heavy gold signet ring on her middle finger smacked against the glass, causing the couple sitting at the window table to stare at her in surprise. 'Ouch!' She hugged the hand to her chest.

Fletcher mouthed an apology to the couple in the restaurant then turned back to Cynthia.

'You are an amazing person, Cynthia. You're going to go far with the company. I know you've been through a tough time recently... outside of work, but it will pass.'

She glared at him now, her eyes burning with indignation.

'You think I want to sleep with you to get back at my ex?'

Fletcher swallowed hard. He didn't want to offend her, but he had heard on the office grapevine that her boyfriend had strayed with her best friend and that Cynthia had been crushed by the double deceit. Also, aside from the fact that theirs was a business relationship, and Fletcher had never wanted – and would never want – to push those professional boundaries, he loved his wife and had no desire to cheat on her. That said, Cynthia was a human being in pain, and he wanted to help if he could.

'I'm not entirely sure what you want, Cynthia. I just don't think this is a good idea.'

'Why not?'

'One, you're my colleague. Two, you're hurting. Three, and most importantly for me, I love my wife.'

Cynthia's face contorted then as myriad emotions crossed her features. Fletcher could see her pain, confusion, fear, sadness and disappointment, and he wished he could take them all away for her. But she was strong, she would survive, and she would come back stronger than ever.

'You've been married for... like, ever.' She tugged at an earlobe. 'Aren't you bored?"

'I have been married for a long time, yes. And Roxie is the most important person in the world to me. I would never betray her trust by cheating.'

'Oh.' Cynthia seemed to deflate in front of him.

'You deserve someone who'll love and adore you, who will treat you well. But first, Cynthia, you need to love yourself.'

Her nostrils flared. 'Don't patronise me!'

Fletcher held up his hands. 'I'm not, I promise. It's something I've heard my wife telling her friends and it seems like sage advice. Don't you think?'

Cynthia closed her eyes for a moment and swayed gently in the afternoon breeze. Fletcher wondered if he was going to have to catch her, but she opened her eyes again and her face adopted the professional mask he knew so well.

'You're absolutely right, Fletcher. It is good advice.' She sighed, then her eyes widened with panic.

'What is it?'

Her face turned green.

'I'm going to be s—'

Then she vomited all over Fletcher's shiny black shoes, sending the stench of wine and garlic up into the air and making him grimace.

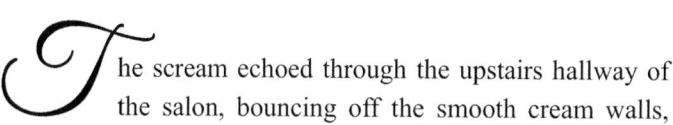

The scream echoed through the upstairs hallway of the salon, bouncing off the smooth cream walls, and Roxie dropped her phone, wincing as it landed with a clatter on the wooden floor.

The door to the beauty room opened and Lila ran out wearing just her underwear. She looked around wildly and her gaze landed on Roxie.

'You!' She pointed a trembling finger at Roxie. 'You did this to me.'

'What?' Roxie picked up her phone then stood up straight. 'What do you mean?' Her heart was racing, her mouth dry.

'You told me it wouldn't hurt.'

'The waxing?'

'What else?' Lila's eyes were glistening, and her lower lip wobbled. 'It did hurt. *A lot!* Like having my hair ripped out.'

'But you were having hair ripped out.' Roxie held out her hands, keeping her voice low and calm as if speaking to a distressed child. 'And I did tell you it would sting.'

'*Sting*!' Lila spat the word at Roxie. 'Like ten thousand wasps. I thought you meant it would sting like… like… Oh, I don't know.' She turned to the beautician who had followed her from the room. 'What really stings?'

'Waxing?' the woman asked, shrugging apologetically.

'Ahhhh!' Lila stamped her feet a few times then turned back to Roxie. 'That was the most painful thing I've ever experienced.'

'You do get used to it.' Roxie felt suddenly very inadequate, as if her words were a few raindrops falling on parched earth. 'How much have you had done?'

Lila looked down at herself then and seemed to realise she was standing in the hallway in just her pink bra and navy knickers.

'Just the one side of my bikini line.' Lila pointed at the very red patch of skin. 'I'm all uneven.'

Roxie averted her gaze as a snort of laughter burst from her. She pressed her free hand to her mouth, trying to hold it in, but it was just too funny. Lila had one red stripe to the left of her knickers and one rather fuzzy side to the right.

'You could leave it like that.' Roxie gritted her teeth together to try to stop the laughter but behind Lila, the beautician had fat tears rolling down her cheeks, streaking her thick foundation.

'I can't exactly go to the lido tomorrow like this, can I?' Lila's lips wavered then she started to laugh. 'Everyone will stare.'

'You might start a new trend. The asymmetrical bikini wax.' Roxie bent over as laughter gripped her and soon she and Lila were on their knees, giggling until their faces ached. 'You could... wear... shorts.' The idea made them laugh even harder.

'I'd better get back in there,' Lila said when she finally managed to catch her breath.

'You better had.' Roxie patted her arm. 'It does get easier though, I promise.'

'If it doesn't, I'm just going to buy a wetsuit and wear that instead.'

Roxie hugged her aching belly as the beautician ushered Lila back into the room.

When she sat back down, she remembered that she'd dropped her phone and checked the screen thoroughly for any damage, but it seemed fine. Fletcher's handsome face smiled at her from the lock screen and she smiled back. For so long now, he had been her rock, her lighthouse, her reason for everything. She loved him deeply and wanted his happiness even before her own. They'd had rough times, sure, but that was what marriage was all about; taking the good with the bad, riding the waves.

In that moment, she wanted to speak to him with a yearning that she hadn't felt in some time, and the thought of waiting until he got home later that evening was unbearable. Surely it would be okay to phone him? Just to say a very quick hello?

She swiped the screen and pressed favourites, then raised the phone to her ear, already imagining the familiar sound of his voice and the warmth and reassurance it would bring.

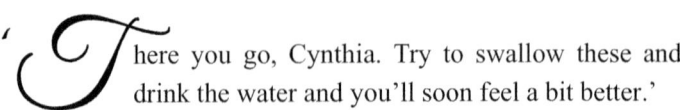

'There you go, Cynthia. Try to swallow these and drink the water and you'll soon feel a bit better.'

Cynthia eyed the paracetamols then the glass of water as if Fletcher had just given her cyanide capsules and a glass of bleach, then emitted a loud burp and Fletcher jumped backwards, fearing a repeat performance of her projectile vomit outside the restaurant. He'd managed to get her back to Bishopsgate and had left her sitting on the sofa in his office while he'd gone to find something to help ease her headache. He'd also been keen to change his trousers and clean his shoes after

Cynthia had pebble dashed them with her lunch, but even though he'd scrubbed at the leather of his brogues, he was sure he could still smell the regurgitated wine and garlicky pasta.

Cynthia now looked less green but a bit pasty and clammy. What she really needed was to go and sleep it off, and when she was steadier on her feet, Fletcher would encourage her to make her way home and start the weekend early. She could claim that she had eaten something that upset her stomach to avoid any repercussions from work. Fletcher just hoped that she'd be okay because when she sobered up properly, she was probably going to feel rather embarrassed.

'Oh…' She raised a finger in the air as if pointing at the ceiling. Her eyes were dark with smudged mascara and her eyebrows appeared to be uneven, which Fletcher found quite disconcerting. 'While you were gone, your phone rang.'

'Did it?' Fletcher patted his trouser pockets then realised he'd left his phone on his desk because he intended on changing in the toilets and didn't want to drop it or leave it there.

'Yes.' Cynthia nodded. 'I answered it.'

Fletcher nodded. 'Okaaay. So… who was it?'

'Roxie.'

'Right. Uh… Did she leave a message?'

Cynthia frowned then rubbed her eyes, spreading the mascara further, but Fletcher's growing unease made him want to ask her to hurry up and tell him what Roxie had said.

'She asked where you were.'

'What did you say?'

'That you were getting changed.'

'Dear god!' Fletcher sighed. Roxie wasn't the jealous or suspicious type, but for a woman to answer his phone then tell his wife that he wasn't around because he was getting changed could well cause problems for the most secure of marriages. 'Did you by any chance explain *why* I was getting changed?'

Cynthia's eyebrows rose. 'Of course not. I don't want your wife thinking I make a habit of going out and getting drunk during lunchtime. Whatever would she think about the people you work with?'

Fletcher retrieved his phone from the desk and peered at the screen, then scrolled to the call list. Roxie's call had lasted two minutes and twenty seconds, enough time for her to put one and one together and end up with five. He pushed his forefinger down his collar and pulled it away from his throat.

'Cynthia… I need to call her back. Would you uh… would you be all right now to go back to your desk?'

She nodded then picked up the glass of water and her bag, and went to the door.

'Fletcher, I am sorry for reading you… us… the situation incorrectly. You were right, things haven't been easy for me lately, but even so… I guess I just thought you seemed lonely too.'

He watched as she left the office and the door closed slowly with a swish, then he slumped onto the sofa. It had been one hell of an afternoon and he couldn't wait to get home and see Roxie, to hold her in his arms and tell her how much he loved her. In fact, he needed to speak to her right now and find out what she was thinking about why one of his female colleagues had answered his phone and told her that he was getting changed, without explaining exactly why.

If it had been the other way around, then Fletcher knew he would have some questions, even if he would (he hoped) be quite certain that it was all completely innocent.

He scrolled to Roxie's number and waited for the call to connect.

4

Roxie followed Lila down the stairs at the salon to the reception desk and they both paid for their treatments. She had barely felt the sting of being waxed, had almost welcomed the distraction from her inner turmoil.

Why had Fletcher been getting changed on a Friday afternoon? Why had a female colleague – one she'd heard mentioned several times over the years as Fletcher had recounted his days over dinner – answered his phone *while* he'd been getting changed? Roxie had been so surprised when a woman had answered Fletcher's mobile that she'd been temporarily struck dumb, then when she'd found her voice, she'd asked where Fletcher was. For one terrifying moment, she'd worried that he'd been taken ill or involved in an accident and a passer-by had picked up his phone, but when she'd asked whom she was speaking to, the woman had told her that it was Cynthia and that she worked with Fletcher. Roxie had asked if her husband was all right and Cynthia had replied that he was fine but getting changed. Cynthia hadn't volunteered any further information, had seemed a bit frosty if anything, as if Roxie had inconvenienced her by calling. Roxie had become flustered and ended the call by asking Cynthia to tell Fletcher that she'd called.

So what had been going on?

Was Fletcher having an affair with a colleague?

It all seemed too preposterous to contemplate, and yet… it happened. It had happened to Lila; beautiful, young, sweet Lila who was standing right next to her. Lila's fiancé had cheated on her before they'd even got down the aisle and he'd been cheating for months. If it could happen to Lila, then surely it could happen to anyone?

But… this was Fletcher. The man who had slept next to her for over twenty years, who had held her hair back when she'd suffered from morning sickness and who had rubbed her feet when they'd ached after a night dancing in heels, who had told her he'd always take care of her and who had worked so hard all the years of their marriage to give her everything she wanted. They had built a home together, laughed and cried together, relied on each other through good times and bad, and he was her best friend in the whole world. He was, quite simply, also her favourite person in the whole world.

The thought that he could have betrayed her trust was far too awful to consider, so she wouldn't. She'd push it from her mind and no doubt, when Fletcher came home later on, he'd have a good explanation for what had happened. It would all be a terrible misunderstanding and Roxie would feel reassured, happy and secure again.

Wouldn't she?

Her phone started to ring so she checked the screen. *Fletcher.* Her heart sank as she rejected the call then turned her phone off. She didn't feel ready to have a conversation with him right now and didn't trust herself not to ask any awkward questions. It would be better to wait until he came home, when would have calmed down and could look at his face and evaluate his reactions. She dropped her phone into her bag.

'Ready Roxie?' Lila asked as she hooked her bag over her shoulder.

'Yes, I'm ready.' Roxie nodded. 'Are you?'

Lila grimaced. 'I feel like I've been whizzed in a blender, but the beautician promised the aloe vera gel will ease the discomfort and that tomorrow I'll feel like a million dollars.'

'I'm sure you will.' Roxie smiled.

'But for now… I'm going to have to walk like a cowboy.'

'A cowboy?' Roxie asked as they went out of the door and down the steps to the street.

'Yes.' Lila nodded. 'Like this.'

Roxie's worries drifted away, pushed to the back of her mind, as she watched her friend walk along the pavement, legs akimbo as if she'd been riding a horse all day. Poor Lila had been initiated into the world of waxing and Roxie could only hope that she would appreciate the results tomorrow.

For today, at least, there was aloe vera gel and a bag of frozen peas waiting in Roxie's freezer.

'Come on, Lila, come back to mine and we'll get you sorted.'

'Thank you.' Lila took Roxie's arm and they plodded along the street together, giggling at Lila's inability to walk with her feet close together.

~

After he had closed the front door behind him, Fletcher put his briefcase down on the dresser in the hallway then he kicked off his shoes and wiggled his toes.

'That feels incredible,' he said, as his aching feet spread out on the cool tiles.

He shrugged out of his suit jacket and draped it over the banister then padded through to the open-plan kitchen-diner.

'What a day that was!' he exclaimed as he went straight to the fridge and grabbed a bottle of beer then twisted off the cap. He took a swig and sighed as the cool beer chilled his mouth and soothed his dry throat. 'Roxie?' He looked around, realising that his wife wasn't in the kitchen.

There was no answer, so he wandered through the ground floor, calling her name. Something else was strange, too. Glenda usually came to greet him when he got home, and he hadn't heard her bark of delight or the skittering of her claws on the tiles as she tried to gain purchase so she could rush to him and jump at his legs.

'Glenda?'

He held his breath, listening for his wife and their dog, but there wasn't a sound in the house except for the beer fizzing in the bottle and the clock ticking in the hallway.

Roxie must have taken Glenda for a walk or to see one of her friends. It was a bit unusual, as she was normally home when he got back from work. It wasn't that he expected her to be there, but she usually was, and if not, she'd let him know. His stomach clenched as he thought about the fact that he hadn't been able to get through to her mobile earlier, and he wondered if it had anything to do with Cynthia answering his phone. Perhaps it had upset or worried Roxie and she hadn't wanted to speak to him. He knew she'd had a beautician appointment that day though, so if she was getting waxed or massaged or whatever else it was that she did there, then it was feasible that she'd turn her phone off. As long as she was okay and not upset or worried. He'd hate for her to be either of those.

He took another swig of his beer then headed up the stairs and across the landing. As he went, he admired the new wallpaper, a pale green affair with cream and silver swirls that made him think of clear springs and summer days. Roxie really did have fantastic taste and Ethan was doing a good job of decorating.

In the master bedroom, he placed his beer on a coaster on his bedside table and undid his tie then dropped it on the bed. He'd take a shower and wash the day away then go down and see what he could make them for dinner.

Perhaps he'd ask if Roxie fancied going out somewhere, they could dress up and go for a nice drive on this lovely evening, find a country pub that did bar meals. He didn't really feel like going out, his back was aching and the idea of a night in front of the TV, snuggled up with his wife appealed far more, but he'd do anything to make Roxie happy and if that meant putting in some effort, even if it was at the end of a very busy working week, he'd happily do it.

He went through to the en suite and turned on the shower. While he undressed, he wondered what time Roxie would get home, hoping she wouldn't be long because he was really missing her today.

~

Roxie kissed Lila's cheek then leant down and clipped Glenda's lead to her harness.

'Are you sure you're all right now, Lila?' she asked.

Lila nodded. 'Thanks for the frozen peas and aloe vera gel. They definitely helped. You really didn't need to walk me home though.'

'It's no problem at all. I couldn't let you do the cowboy walk alone, could I? Besides which, Glenda needed a walk.'

Glenda had needed a walk but so had Roxie. She'd been unable to bear the thought of waiting for Fletcher to get home because she knew that she'd get wound up, especially if he was late. She'd checked her voicemail and found that he'd left two messages earlier that afternoon, asking her to call him when she got a chance, but she hadn't wanted to speak to him on the phone. She needed to look into his eyes and to watch his face, to know that he hadn't done anything that would ruin their marriage.

'Ethan would have walked with me,' Lila said.

'I know that.' Roxie nodded. 'But he did need to get back to his mum to take her for that GP check-up.'

'He did.' Lila winced. 'Ooh! I think I'm going to need to soak in a cold bath.'

'It will ease by tomorrow.'

'I hope so!' Lila bit her bottom lip. 'I mean… I can hardly go to the lido if my bikini line is glowing.'

'You'll be fine.' Roxie looked at the clock on Lila's mantelpiece. 'I'd better go. It's almost seven, so Fletcher might be home, or if not, hopefully he soon will be.'

'Okay well have a lovely evening and I'll see you in the morning.'

'I can't wait. It will be a lovely day and a very positive one for the village. The lido has been closed for such a long time, and it was a terrible waste. It will be wonderful to see the community come together to enjoy it.'

Roxie went to the door and let herself and Glenda out.

'See you tomorrow!'

Walking back towards her own house, she sighed. Seeing Fletcher was always something she looked forward to, even after all these years, but this evening she felt a sense of impending doom, as if seeing him would bring her fears to a head. She didn't want to believe that he'd been doing anything with Cynthia, didn't feel able to believe it deep down in her heart, but then she also knew that affairs did happen and that hearts could change.

'Come on, Glenda, shall we see if Daddy's home?' She injected some positivity into her voice and Glenda peered up at her, her mouth open in what reminded Roxie of a big grin.

Roxie forced a smile to her lips, trying to relax her face. Whatever was going on was probably nothing to worry about and nowhere near her worst fears. It was Friday evening and she was going to spend it with her husband; that in itself was a reason to be happy.

～

Fletcher patted some cologne onto his freshly shaven face and smiled at his reflection in the bathroom mirror. He'd shaved, showered and dressed in navy chinos and a pale blue shirt, casual enough to stay home but smart enough should Roxie want to go out for dinner. If not, he'd cook tonight; he wanted her to relax and feel spoilt.

He wiped his hands on a towel hanging on the rail then made his way downstairs. As he reached the ground floor, the front door opened and Glenda ran in, skidding on the tiles when she spotted him. She jumped up at his legs, grinning broadly, and he bent over to rub her head and her soft little ears.

'Hello, Glenda. Have you and Mum been out?'

The dog barked then raced around the hallway, skidding each time she turned, and in spite of his tiredness, Fletcher laughed.

'Oh! You're home.'

Roxie closed the door then placed her keys on the hall table.

'I am. Hello, my beautiful wife.'

Opening his arms wide, he approached her, but she ducked away. His chest squeezed and he tucked his hands into his pockets.

'Sorry.' She held up her hands. 'I just had to pick up a poo so need to wash these before I touch anything.'

He nodded, hoping that was the real reason she had evaded his hug.

In the kitchen, he perched on a stool at the counter while she scrubbed her hands with antibacterial soap. Glenda wandered into the kitchen then over to her bed under the breakfast bar where she found a chew that she started to gnaw.

'How was your day?' Fletcher asked.

'Okay, thanks.' Roxie flashed him a smile but it didn't reach her eyes. 'I took Lila to the beauty salon and she had her first experience of waxing.'

'Ouch!' He laughed then winced, as it sounded false. He was clearly nervous, but he hoped Roxie wouldn't read it as guilt.

'She didn't enjoy it at all.' Roxie flicked her dark hair and it swished across her shoulders and tumbled down over her chest. She was beautiful, amazing and perfect, and Fletcher had to force himself to stay where he was. He could tell that she wasn't in a great mood and knew he shouldn't try to hug her because when Roxie was in a mood, which wasn't often, she liked to have some space.

'Apart from that?' he asked.

She shrugged as she reached for a tube of hand cream on the windowsill then squeezed some onto a palm. As she rubbed it in, she avoided the diamonds in her engagement ring.

'It was okay.' She looked up and met his gaze and something in her green almond-shaped eyes flashed. 'You?'

'Busy one, but not too bad. Glad to be home now though.'

'Right.'

'Roxie…'

'Yes?'

'Today… you rang me. And… someone else picked up.'

'Your colleague Cynthia, I believe.' Her voice was cold, and it made him shiver. He hated for her to think badly of him, had always flourished in her love and admiration.

'Yes. See, the thing is…'

'You don't need to explain. It's your… your …' She knitted her brows together.

'Roxie, there was nothing going on. You know me, you know how much I love you and always have. I've never strayed and never will do.'

'Except when an attractive younger colleague comes on to you?' Her eyes bored into him then. This wasn't like the woman he knew and loved. But he also knew that, in this case, she was almost right. Cynthia had come on to him.

'It wasn't like that.' He felt exhausted, depleted.

'No?' Roxie put her hands on her hips and Fletcher couldn't help admiring how her hips curved outwards from her slim waist, her figure enhanced by the fitted yoga pants and black T-shirt she was wearing. 'So you're telling me that she didn't try it on?'

'What?' He rubbed his neck, feeling the short hairs there grate against his palm. He didn't want to lie to Roxie, yet he knew that telling her the exact truth would be almost as bad, worse probably because it would worry her. 'No. Well, yes.

Kind of… see… We went out for lunch and Cynthia had too much wine and—'

'Wine? During a working lunch?'

'You know that when we take clients out, there's usually wine with the food. It's part of the whole process of wining and dining them to get the best deals, the loyalty…'

'So you were eating with clients?'

'Well… no. Not exactly.'

'Which is it, Fletcher?' Roxie's cheeks were flushed now and her eyebrows had risen almost to her hairline.

'It wasn't a client dinner, but a group of us went out for lunch.'

'A group?'

'Yes. From the office.'

'And Cynthia drank too much?'

'She did.' He pushed himself off the stool and loosened the collar of his shirt, easing the pressure it was exerting on his Adam's apple. 'She didn't feel well so we were heading back to the office but before we got there, she was sick on my shoes and my trousers, and that was why I needed to get changed.'

Roxie folded her arms across her chest and seemed to weigh up what he'd told her. 'Where did you change?'

'In the toilets.'

'While she was in your office?'

'Yes, drinking water and trying to sober up.'

'Okay.' She nodded. 'But she did try it on?'

'A bit. Yes. She… she told me she liked me, and I told her I wasn't interested. She was fine about it.'

'But she vomited on you? Was this before or after?'

'After what?'

'After she told you that she liked you.'

'Oh… after.' Even though he'd showered he was convinced he could still smell Cynthia's pungent vomit and his stomach churned.

Silence fell in the kitchen; even Glenda stopped chewing and peered up at her humans, looking from one to the other like a tennis umpire.

'Is she attractive?'

'Roxie, angel, it doesn't matter.'

'It matters to me. You're working with a woman who thinks it's okay to try to seduce you even though she knows you're married. You see more of her than me probably, so I'd like to know if she's attractive.'

Fletcher sighed and ran his hands through his hair, feeling how it had thinned out recently, how there was far less at the crown than there had been.

'She's all right, I suppose, if you like that kind of… look. But I don't and anyway, she's not a patch on you.'

Roxie seemed to sag in front of him, as if she'd been holding herself tense, and now she could release her fears.

'Okay.' She clutched her hands to her stomach, her chin resting on her chest.

'Are we okay?'

'Yes.' It was barely more than a whisper.

'Would you like to go out for dinner this evening?'

Roxie leant against the apron fronted sink, reached back with her hands and held on to it, as if she needed to hold herself up.

'I have a bit of a headache and I feel exhausted to be honest.' She did look tired. Shadows had appeared below her eyes and her cheeks had hollowed in the time since she'd arrived home. It was as if she'd used all of her energy during their interaction. 'I think I'll have a lie down. You go out if you like… or we can order a takeaway.'

'I'm certainly not going to go out without you. I've missed you and want to spend some time with you, Rox. What would you like to do?'

'You decide. I have to get rid of this headache.' Roxie went to the kitchen door. 'I'll see you in a bit.'

She left the kitchen and Fletcher's heart sank to the cold tiled floor. He couldn't remember the last time he'd felt so awful, so inadequate, so alone. Roxie had listened to his version of the story, the version that was the truth, but he wasn't sure if she did believe him. He hated the thought of hurting her, of disappointing her in any way and of her feeling that he'd let her down.

He slumped to the tiles next to Glenda's bed and stroked her soft fur. She rolled onto her back, offering him her belly to tickle so he obliged, smiling at how her tongue lolled from her mouth when she was relaxed and at how easy it was to make her happy.

If only he could make Roxie that happy too.

He decided he needed to do something to prove to his wife that she was the most important person in the world to him, to show her exactly how much he loved her, and that he would never take her love for granted.

5

'Ugh…' Roxie sat up in bed. Actually, on top of the bed. She was lying on the coverlet with a soft fleece blanket draped over her. And she was still wearing yesterday's clothes. Her mouth was dry, tasted like cough syrup – a floral antiseptic flavour – and her neck was stiff from where she'd slept on decorative pillows that were meant to be removed before getting into bed.

She pushed the blanket back and moved to the edge of the king-size mattress then swung her legs over the side. On the bedside table, she noted the small bottle of herbal sleep aid and recalled taking twice the recommended dose the previous evening.

'Why did I do that?' she asked the empty bedroom.

Where's Fletcher? Glenda? What time is it?

She stood up on shaky legs and hobbled to the en suite. Turning the cold tap on, she splashed some water over her face before drinking some straight from the tap. In the mirror above the sink, she saw that her eyes were bloodshot with dark shadows underneath and she grimaced. She looked bloody awful, as if she'd been whitewashed overnight and borrowed someone else's eye bags to carry her luggage. Or was that baggage... of the emotional kind? Her hair was sticking up at her parting as if she'd backcombed it before bed and she had a trickle of dried drool down her chin that glistened like a snail trail.

She rubbed at it with a wet hand and dried her face on a towel.

Then she froze.

Because everything that happened yesterday came flooding back. It felt like standing at the end of a corridor then being hurtled backwards on roller skates at sixty miles an hour. She leant forwards and dry-heaved over the sink until she knew for certain that nothing was going to come up.

When she had come home from Lila's, Fletcher had been in the kitchen. They had talked, or he had tried to talk, but Roxie hadn't really felt ready to discuss why another woman had answered his phone. She'd felt unable to digest Fletcher's explanation, had needed some time to mull it over. In the cold light of day, it seemed a bit immature of her to walk away, but she'd felt indescribably angry, in spite of his apologetic tone, and had needed to put some space between them so she wouldn't say anything she'd regret. She loved her husband and didn't want to hurt him or say mean things to him, so walking away had seemed better. She'd also had the headache from hell and felt as though her skull would split in two if she didn't rest.

Upstairs, she'd rubbed her throbbing temples, gone to the en-suite cabinet to find some headache tablets and come across the herbal sleep remedy. A nap had seemed like a good idea, so she'd slugged some of the mixture and that was the last thing she remembered. Fletcher must have come upstairs at some point and covered her with the blanket.

Had he tried to wake her? Had he slept next to her? Was he even home?

Suddenly, the yearning to see him was overwhelming and she rushed through the bedroom and down the stairs, skidding across the hallway towards the lounge.

And there he was. Stretched out on the sofa with Glenda at his feet. Both of them snoring gently.

She approached cautiously, not wanting to disturb them, and looked down at his face. In sleep, he looked far younger than his forty-nine years, his forehead broad and clear, the fine lines at his eyes smoothed away, his lips slightly parted. He was a handsome man, she had always been proud to be by his side, and after all the years together, she could see it still. Even with the slight paunch he'd developed from eating so well and enjoying the odd drink or two, he was still the man she adored. But it was more than just his looks; Fletcher was intelligent, compassionate, funny, sharp, erudite, accomplished and yet he was humble too.

She could see why other women would find him attractive. The thought was like a knife to her gut and she winced. Other women... *like Cynthia*. Fletcher had said nothing untoward had happened, that he had no interest in anyone else, but even so, Roxie now knew that Cynthia wanted more from Fletcher, had tried to get more. Jealousy pierced her heart like an arrow, and she gasped, shocked at its intensity. It was an unfamiliar and unwelcome emotion and she willed it to pass.

Bile burned her throat, so she picked up the empty whisky tumbler from the coffee table and tiptoed away, not wanting to cry and wake her husband and dog. She'd make some coffee and throw some of those frozen croissants in the oven so breakfast would be ready for Fletcher when he woke. He could probably do with a restful morning; he worked so hard, got so tired, deserved some kindness.

In the kitchen, she boiled the kettle, turned the oven on and put two croissants in then went to the breakfast bar and sat on a stool to wait. As she sat down, she spotted Fletcher's mobile on the worktop in front of her. She reached for it, meaning to check the time.

It was only six-thirty-five a.m. No wonder she still felt bone weary.

She put the phone back down and stretched her arms above her head, trying to loosen the knots in her neck and shoulders.

Then the phone buzzed.

And a notification flashed on the screen.

She saw the name Cynthia and the first line of a message before the screen went black again.

Morning!
Need to speak to you.
Call me… X

Roxie's stomach churned. Why was Cynthia texting Fletcher so early in the morning and why did she need to speak to him? More to the point, why the hell was there a kiss at the end of the message if Cynthia was simply a colleague?

She sprang from the stool, marched from the kitchen and up the stairs. There was no way she was going to sit around and be taken for a fool. She'd be gone before her husband woke and he could see how it felt to rattle around the house all alone for a change.

As she packed a bag to take to the lido, then dressed quickly, she flicked tears away from her eyes. She wouldn't weaken, wouldn't collapse on the floor in a snotty heap, wouldn't let this beat her.

So what if a younger, hotter woman was chasing Fletcher. So what if he was flattered. So what if... if nothing was going on. What was that saying? *There's no smoke without fire...* And right now, Roxie could smell smoke.

She paused.

She actually could smell smoke.

Shit! The croissants!

She grabbed her bag, stuffed her feet into sandals and hurried downstairs to the kitchen. She dropped her bag, switched the oven off and opened the door.

'A bit bloody late!' she said as the smoke alarm rang through the house. She dropped her bag, switched the oven off and opened the door then fanned a frying pan in front of the open oven, holding her breath, her eyes watering.

When the smoke had finally cleared, she stuck her hand in an oven glove and carried the tray of burnt pastries out to the garden then set it on the patio table. The croissants resembled burnt slugs, small and shrivelled, a bit like her heart felt right now.

She shrugged. Well, that was that then. Fletcher would have to have something else for his breakfast and he could bloody well make it himself too.

Back inside, she frowned at the smell, then spotted Glenda in the doorway looking perplexed, her small head leaning to one side.

'It's okay, baby. You hungry?'

She got Glenda's meat from the fridge – she fed the pug the raw diet after reading that it helped eliminate yeast issues, which Glenda was prone to – and filled a bowl then set it down.

'You eat and wake-up a bit and Mummy will be back for you later.'

She picked up her bag and left the kitchen.

In the hallway she found a bleary-eyed Fletcher, blinking up at the alarm on the ceiling.

'Morning,' she said, and his gaze moved to her. In his navy and white checked pyjama bottoms and pale blue T-shirt, he looked so adorable that she almost lost her composure and ran to him. But she forced the image of the text into her mind and held it there.

She had to be sensible about all of this.

She had to be strong.

'Morning, Rox. You okay?'

'Hmmm.' She pressed her lips together.

'You going somewhere?' He gestured at her white jeans, pink blouse and sandals. 'You look lovely, very summery.'

'I'm going to Lila's for breakfast then we're off to the lido.'

'Oh yeah, that's opening today, isn't it?'

'Yes, today is the grand opening. I put croissants in the oven for you, but they burnt so you'll have to have cereal or something.' She gave a carefree flick of her wrist, although everything inside her was screaming in protest. The idea of leaving Fletcher to sort out his own breakfast went against everything she'd become accustomed to. He went out to work and she looked after things at home, she made him meals and did his washing and ironing, kept their home nice, appreciated how hard he worked. He was, in all fairness, always grateful and appreciative of her efforts and it had, over the years, given her great pleasure to do nice things for him.

They loved each other. Their balance, if a bit old-fashioned to some people, worked. Or had worked.

She covered her mouth as a sob escaped.

'What is it Roxie?' He approached her holding out a hand, but she stepped backwards. She knew that if he touched her, she would unravel and she needed time to think, to process what had happened yesterday as well as what she'd just seen on his phone.

'Don't.' She held up a hand. 'Please don't.'

He frowned and rubbed at his stubble. Even that sound made her long to touch him, to press her nose to his jaw and breathe him in. She loved his scent, especially in the mornings when they'd just woken up. It was all him, masculine and rousing, familiar and comforting.

This man was everything to her.

He had been everything to her throughout her adult life.

And now something was threatening to come between them.

'I have to go. I'll see you later.'

'Please don't rush off, Roxie. Let's talk.'

His tone was filled with hurt and confusion.

'We can talk but not yet. First you need to go and look at your phone.'

'What?'

'And before you think I've been going through it, I haven't. I checked the time on it and put it down then a message alert came through.'

'From who?'

Roxie tried to say the name, tried to force her lips into saying the C at least, but her mouth wouldn't cooperate.

'Just take a look.'

'Okay, I will. But Rox…'

'Yes?'

'Take care today. When will you be home?'

She swallowed hard, shrugged, then shifted her bag to a more comfortable position on her shoulder. 'Later. I'm not sure when. I won't be late.'

'Have a good time.'

'Thanks.'

She went to the front door and opened it.

'Roxy? Please remember that I love you.'

She gave a sharp nod then stepped out into the morning and closed the door, just as the tears started to fall.

~

Fletcher traipsed towards the kitchen with Glenda at his heels. He made a coffee, grabbed his phone then opened the back door and headed out into the garden.

It was a beautiful morning; still early enough that beads of dew coated the ground and outdoor furniture. He brushed a hand over one of the seat cushions and sat down, feeling the damp seeping into his pyjama bottoms but failing to care. Glenda sat at his feet, her little back legs resting to one side in a way that made her resemble a human. Even in his current sombre mood, Glenda's funny ways made him smile.

He sipped his coffee then sat back, watching as steam rose from the mug into the cool air. The garden was private and one of the things that had led to them buying the house many years ago. The high walls that provided privacy and security, along with plenty of land providing the potential to grow trees and flowers, herbs and vegetables, had appealed immensely to their younger selves. Fletcher could even recall times when, during their early days at the house, he and Roxie had come outside and made love under the stars. No one could see into their garden and they'd been young, daring and delighted with each other. Back then, their love had been cemented by their mutual commitment, by their need to spend hours kissing and exploring each other, finding things about each other emotionally and physically that would surprise and enchant them. Things that would bind them together for a lifetime.

When did that all change?

As other things crept in, like tiredness after a working day and a long week, when bills needed to be paid and emails answered, even in the evening. When there were meetings to prepare for and early trains to catch to ensure that presentations ran on time. When an unwelcome sense of disillusionment crept into their marriage like a ghoul, making them both wonder if the other cared as much as before, if they found each other as attractive as they once did, if there was still a real connection between them like there used to be or if it had been lost along the way.

Sadness stole through him, making his limbs heavy and his heart ache. When he'd first met Roxie, he'd fallen in love with her and been swept along on a wave of passion and love, sworn to her and himself that she would always be his number one, his reason for everything, his soulmate. He had been convinced that he would show her every day how much he adored her, that he would never take her for granted or allow her to feel unwanted or insignificant. And yet, somehow, it had happened; time and life had worn away at them and now there was a chasm between them, a chasm where both of them were teetering on the edge. They could lose their balance and slip in at any moment and their marriage would be swallowed whole, their relationship disappearing into the darkness.

Without Roxie, life would be empty, meaningless and bleak. She was his best friend, his happiness, his comfort, his other half. Love like theirs didn't come along by chance, it was discovered and then worked on, nurtured like the plants in the garden. It had to be tended to, brought to the forefront and treasured. The alternative was unthinkable, and yet they had allowed it to happen.

Was it too late?

Fletcher hoped not. Their bond was still there, resilient if shaky. It had to be worth fighting for.

Aromas of roses and honeysuckle permeated the air and he breathed deeply of them, enjoying their sweet natural scent. Roxie was a keen gardener and had cultivated their garden into a place of beauty over the years, a place they seldom appreciated anymore because they were so busy, or at least Fletcher was so busy. Too busy. *What a fool...*

He leant forwards and rubbed Glenda's head and she peered up at him, her big eyes filled with love and trust.

'You know what, Glenda?'

She sniffed his hand then gave it a lick and her soft tongue tickled his palm.

'It's time now, at last, to wake-up and literally smell the roses. I need to show your mum exactly how much I love her because without her...' His throat tightened and he took a few deep breaths to ease the discomfort. 'For me, there is no life without Roxie. She has, and always will be, my everything.'

Remembering what she had said about his phone, he picked it up and scrolled through his messages. Then he saw the one that Cynthia had sent this morning.

What the hell does she want now?

No wonder Roxie had become upset. This was exactly what they didn't need, especially after yesterday. He dropped the phone on the table and buried his head in his hands, pressing his fingertips into his scalp.

When he felt a bit calmer, he sat up again and drank the rest of his coffee, pushed himself to his feet and headed back inside. He wasn't entirely sure what he was going to do but he needed to give it some thought.

Winning back his wife's trust and affection was his main priority and he wouldn't let anything get in the way.

6
---

*I*t was only a short walk from Lila's cottage to the thick stone walls that surrounded the local lido. For years, the lido and its grounds had been closed to the public and almost forgotten, like a castle in a fairy tale, as ivy grew thick on the walls and the padlock rusted on the heavy iron gates. For some local teenagers, the grounds had been somewhere to go on a dare. Roxie had heard stories of those who climbed over the walls under cover of darkness to take their chances in the pitch-black area within, but the pool had remained empty, so there'd been no chance of a swim, and apart from local wildlife, there had been nothing within the walls to terrify the teens.

Then, about two years ago, a woman from Devon, Katie Bryant, moved to the village and bought a run-down property. She did the house up and decided to settle there. Roxie knew her to say hello to and not much more, but had heard on the village grapevine that Katie had an impressive résumé of renovating properties and was, therefore, quite well off. Having finished her work on the house, Katie then set about getting the right permissions to bring the lido back to life. A generous donation from her, along with some fundraising and donations from local businesses, as well as a private investor, had meant that within just over a year, the lido and grounds had been restored to their former glory. Roxie had seen photographs in the promotional materials but had yet to see the transformation in person, although she had heard that it was nothing short of magnificent.

Outside the new shiny gates, Lila and Roxie smiled at the pretty teenaged girl standing behind a folding table. Braces shone on her teeth and her brown hair bounced in a high ponytail. Her eyes were hidden behind reflective aviator sunglasses.

'Do you have your tickets?' she asked.

'Yes.' Roxie pulled her purse from her bag and got the two tickets out. She'd purchased them weeks ago at the library, keen to secure entry on opening day. As a bonus, a previously purchased ticket came with a free drink and entry into a raffle. Katie had put an announcement in the village paper informing people that there should be enough tickets available for everyone, and that if they didn't manage to get one, they could pay at the gate, but Roxie hadn't wanted to chance it.

Roxie handed the tickets to the teenager then smiled as the girl gestured for her and Lila to go through the turnstile that had been erected just inside of the main gate.

'Have a great day, ladies!' the girl said.

'Thanks,' Lila replied.

'We will.' Roxie flashed her a grin.

'Well, this is exciting.' Lila touched Roxie's arm after they'd passed through the turnstile.

'It is.' Roxie nodded, but her heart was heavy, and she felt weighed down by sadness. She hoped it would pass because she'd looked forward to this day ever since she'd heard about the reopening. Of course, ideally, Fletcher would have come too but when she'd mentioned it a few weeks ago, he laughed then said, 'Not really my cup of tea, Rox, being surrounded by local kids and sulky teens. You go with a friend. You'll enjoy it more.' It had grated on Roxie for about ten minutes then she'd swallowed her disappointment and imagined herself going with Lila instead.

'Are you all right?' Lila asked, peering at Roxie's face but the huge sunglasses she'd donned to hide her red eyes meant that Lila wouldn't be able to tell.

'I'm fine, Lila. You know me… always smiling.'

'Yes, but… I do worry about you… and, well… did anything happen last night to upset you? You don't have to tell me, but you can if you want to.'

'I know I can and thank you. But…' Roxie blew out her cheeks and pushed her shoulders back. 'I want us to have a good day, to relax, smile, swim and then dry off in the sun. So, let's forget our worries and just have a good time.'

'Of course. But if you want to talk at any point, I'm here for you.'

'Thank you.'

Roxie slid her arm through Lila's, and they made their way along the gravel path to the steps that led up to the pool area. Music floated through the air, a once very popular tune by

George Michael. It made goosebumps rise on Roxie's arms as it brought back memories of times when she'd danced to it with Fletcher, when he'd held her tight against his chest and kissed her forehead then whispered to her about how much he loved her. Behind her sunglasses she blinked hard, determined not to let the tears fall.

They climbed the wide stone steps flanked by thick carved stone pillars, presumably the originals that had been lovingly restored, and Roxie caught the whiff of chlorine on the gentle breeze.

At the top of the steps, the pool area came into view and they both gasped. Lush green grass gave way to a paved area where wooden sunloungers with fat yellow cushions were set out in rows under large umbrellas in a rainbow of colours. Off to the left was another set of steps that led up to a shop, a bar and another seating area, while to the right was a small park with swings, slides, a seesaw and a sandpit. Children and adults had been well catered for.

In front of them, at the centre of the paved area, was the pool itself. At fifty metres, it was huge, and it beckoned to them, a blue lagoon where they could swim, relax and unwind, where they could immerse themselves and let their cares and worries float away.

'Shall we go and get some sunloungers?' Lila asked.

Roxie nodded. Part of the reason they'd come so early was to get somewhere to sit, or at least that was what Roxie had told Lila when she'd turned up on her doorstep first thing in the morning.

They headed for the sunloungers at the far end of the pool, where they'd have just a short walk up to the bar. Not that

Roxie planned on drinking and swimming, but it would be nice to get some chilled soft drinks as the day warmed up.

Once they had spread out their towels, they sat down and looked around. There were a few people milling around the grounds, taking a look at the trees and plants, some familiar faces and some new ones, while others made their way up to the shop and bar. On the opposite side of the pool, a young couple rubbed sun cream onto each other, giggling and flirting, clearly enjoying being together. Roxie and Fletcher had been like that once, unable to stop touching and kissing, staring into each other's eyes, wanting to spend every waking moment together.

When had that changed?

Roxie leant forwards, slid her hands behind her knees and squeezed her eyes closed behind her sunglasses. How did a couple go from being so devoted and completely in love to being almost indifferent, to taking things like spending sunny days together for granted to the extent that they rarely did so? Fletcher could have been here with her today, but he had basically scoffed at the idea, presumably preferring the prospect of a round of golf with some of the men he knew from the club to a day of swimming and sunning himself with his wife. It hurt Roxie to think about it, so she often didn't, and she realised she'd become accustomed to accepting that their relationship had changed so drastically. It hadn't happened overnight but crept up on them gradually, one change at a time, so they were now at a stage of disconnect. It was a dangerous stage, one where other people could seem attractive, where affairs could happen…

Was that what had happened with Fletcher and Cynthia? Did she appeal to him as a possible connection, as a preferable alternative to Roxie who was simply a reminder of what they had lost?

'Look at that!' Lila broke into her thoughts and Roxie followed her pointing finger. Katie Bryant was strolling around the poolside carrying what looked like a picnic basket. Every time she reached someone, she stopped, spoke to them, then handed them something from the basket. 'What's she giving them?'

'I guess we'll find out.' Roxie peered over her sunglasses as Katie approached.

'Hello, ladies. I'm so glad you could make it today.' Katie smiled at them, flashing teeth that could have belonged to a Hollywood star.

Smiling up at the younger woman, Roxie admired how classy she looked in a white short-sleeved blouse and tight white jeans paired with cork wedges. An oval silver locket hung around her neck and silver bangles jangled on her left wrist. Her dark wavy hair hung around her shoulders, the sun catching the caramel and gold streaks and her brown eyes crinkled endearingly at the corners as she smiled.

'We're delighted to be here,' Roxie said. 'This will be such a good thing for the community.'

Katie nodded. 'That's what I thought. Good for the children and future generations too. Bella is overjoyed by it all.'

Bella was Katie's ten-year-old daughter. She lived in the village with Katie but there was no man on the scene. Roxie had heard that Katie had been married but didn't know much else about it and Katie seemed to keep her personal life and history private, which was, of course, her right.

'Where is Bella?' Lila asked.

'Here somewhere.' Katie laughed. 'Probably bossing one of her friends around or giving someone directions. No doubt she'll be offering swimming lessons soon. She's like a mermaid, a proper water baby.'

'Are you expecting a lot of people here today?'

'Definitely.' Katie nodded. 'And all the profits will go towards the upkeep of the lido and to making it accessible for all.' She gestured broadly at the landscape and Roxie spotted the wheelchair ramps and pool lift that she hadn't noticed before.

'Wonderful.' Lila smiled. 'And what about dogs?'

'Sorry.' Katie frowned.

'Will dogs be allowed in the grounds?'

'Oh, yes, of course. But they must be kept on leads at all times and… sadly… they're not allowed in the pool. However, there are drinking stations for them dotted around the grounds and up at the shop they sell doggy frozen yogurt in a variety of fruity flavours.'

'Wow, you've thought of everything.' Roxie was impressed.

'This is a community lido, so I wanted people to feel comfortable here. I'm hoping we can hold swimming galas, school events and host things like parent and baby groups, OAP sessions, and possibly even a village mini Olympic games.'

'That all sounds great.' Roxie could imagine the villagers competing in swimming races and the local children having swimming lessons at the pool. It was all so positive and exciting. Her own children might even have taken part.

She swallowed hard, grief scratching at her throat like sandpaper.

'Anyway... I wanted to give you one of these.'

Katie handed them both a metal straw from the basket she was carrying. 'We want to be as environmentally friendly as possible here, so there will be no plastic straws or packaging wherever possible. If you want a straw, please bring this one with you whenever you visit.'

'Great idea,' Lila said.

'It was Bella's idea, actually.' Katie beamed with maternal pride. 'My daughter is a true eco-warrior. Right... if I don't get a chance to speak to you later, have a wonderful day! Oh and before I forget, Stuart Philpot is going to officially open the lido.'

Katie walked away, and Lila turned to Roxie. 'Stuart Philpot? That name's familiar... I think he might have been friendly with Ben or did Ben dislike him?' She frowned.

'Stuart is our local minor celeb,' Roxie explained. 'The one who had a small part on that TV series about a cult in Manchester?'

Lila's frown deepened.

'A cult?'

'Yes, he wasn't in the cult, but he had a younger sister who was.'

'In the series?

'Yes.'

'Oh, right.' Lila nodded. 'That's who I was thinking of. He's big…' She raised her shoulders up to her ears and folded her hands into her armpits. 'Very muscular and he's always tanned.'

'That's the one. Our very own Vin Diesel lookalike. He's muscular because he takes part in strongman competitions around the world and tanned because he spends a lot of time in Tenerife. In fact, I think he might actually own a pub out there.'

'That's right. Ben definitely did not like him. He had a few drinks with him from time to time at the pub, but to be honest, I think he was a bit intimidated by him, possibly even jealous.'

'That doesn't surprise me.' Roxie tutted. Lila's ex fiancé, Ben, was not on her list of favourite people. In fact, because of how he'd treated Lila, Roxie hoped she'd never see him in the village again.

'Shall I go and get us a drink?' Lila asked. 'Then we can test out our straws.'

'Good idea.' Roxie nodded. 'I'll stay here and people-watch.'

Lila grabbed her purse then stood up and walked away. Roxie watched her go, her hips swaying in a bright pink cotton sundress with spaghetti straps and a knee-length hem. Her blonde hair was held back from her face by a butterfly clip and it shone like gold in the morning sunlight. Ben hadn't deserved Lila at all, and Roxie was glad that her friend had Ethan now. Ethan was everything that Ben hadn't been and

Roxie felt certain that Lila would have her best summer on Sunflower Street yet.

~

Fletcher closed his laptop and sat back in his chair. He'd had a productive morning of planning and felt happy with what he'd done. He only hoped Roxie would be pleased with it and that it would help to repair things between them. They might have grown apart but he felt sure that with time and patience, as well as a whole load of love and attention, they could repair their connection and be as happy together as they once were. He had also dealt with Cynthia by replying to her text and asking her to leave him alone outside of working hours unless it was an emergency. His phone had pinged almost immediately with her response:

Of course. I understand.
Only wanted to apologise again.
I'm an idiot. :-(

He got up and wandered over to the front window and peered out at the street beyond their front garden. It was a beautiful summer day and he really should try to make the most of it, even if he was tired and achy from a busy week, as well as from holding himself tense because he was so worried.

'Glenda!' he called. It took a few seconds, but he heard her tiny paws pitter-patter across the hallway and she appeared in the lounge doorway. When he'd made a coffee an hour ago, she'd been lying in a patch of sunlight that shone through the kitchen window and warmed the floor tiles. She hadn't moved when he'd come through to the lounge and would probably have stayed there all afternoon if he hadn't called her.

'Fancy a walk?'

Her ears flicked and she ran at him then jumped at his calves, her feet tapping against his pyjamas.

'I'll go and dress then take you out, shall I? We could even go and see Mum at the lido.'

Glenda rewarded him with a bark then she raced off to the stairs, intent on encouraging him to get a move on.

'I'm coming, girl! Don't worry, I won't let you down.'

As he climbed the stairs, he whispered to himself, 'And I won't let you down either, Roxie.'

∽

'Mmm. This mocktail is delicious.' Roxie licked her lips. 'What did you say it was again?'

'It's a virgin mojito.'

'It's really refreshing with the mint and the limes.'

'Be even nicer with rum in it.'

'Maybe later.' Roxie lowered her sunglasses and wiggled her eyebrows at Lila, making her giggle.

The morning had worn on pleasantly, and the grounds of the lido had filled up so that every sunlounger, chair, bench and table was occupied by groups of friends, couples and families. The air was filled with laughter, shouts, squeals of delight and splashing as people swam around in the water, socialised at the poolside and made the most of the beautiful day.

'Lila, you need more cream on your legs. They're a bit pink.'

'Oh right. Oops! It is quite warm now. I think I'll cover up for a bit.'

'How about a swim to cool down first?' Roxie removed her sunglasses and set them on the lounger, then stood up and stripped down to her black swimming costume.

'Wow!' Lila's eyes widened. 'That is what I call *a costume.*'

Roxie laughed. 'I bought it from one of those websites that specialises in swimwear with secret support. It's not too much?'

'Not at all. Has Fletcher seen you wearing it?'

'No.'

'Well, when he does, he won't be able to take his eyes off you.'

Roxie shrugged. Maybe that was true, but then, if he had eyes for a younger woman, it probably wasn't.

But did he have eyes for Cynthia? Was she really competition for Roxie?

She pushed the thoughts away. The black costume fit well; supported her boobs, flattened her tummy and was cut flatteringly to sit high on her hips to make her legs look longer. It also had a low back and showed off all the time she'd spent doing yoga and Pilates, but she hadn't put herself through all that self-care for nothing. Fletcher might never get to see it but wearing it made Roxie feel good and that was what mattered.

'Shall we swim?' she asked Lila.

'Absolutely.'

Lila was already in her bikini, so she removed her sunglasses then stood up and walked with Roxie to the pool. They sat on the edge for a few moments, dangling their legs in the water. It was cool but not cold and Roxie knew that her skin would soon become accustomed to it.

'Here goes!' She moved forwards and slid into the water then gasped as it rushed over her skin, its cold caress making goosebumps pop out on her arms and legs and she fought the urge to wrap her arms around herself.

'I need to do a few lengths,' she said as Lila slid in next to her.

'Me too. Let's go for it.'

They swam up and down in one of the designated swimming lanes, and Roxie enjoyed the rush of moving quickly, using her limbs to propel herself forwards as the water supported her body. She hadn't been swimming in a while and it was invigorating. The scent of the chlorine mixed with coconut sun cream, the glint of the sun on the water's surface, the sight of pale limbs beneath the water and the sounds of happiness all around were uplifting. She wondered how anyone could come to this lovely place and not feel better. And, of course, the endorphins from exercising were kicking in and providing the familiar boost that she had come to love.

When they had swum ten lengths and Roxie's heart was racing, they made their way to the side. They climbed out then sat there, letting the sun warm their skin and dry their hair.

'That was fun.' Lila's cheeks were rosy, her eyes bright.

'It was and you look amazing.'

'Thank you, so do you. We'll have to do this regularly.'

'I'd like that.'

A tinkling sound cut through the afternoon air and all heads turned to an area on the grass where a small raised platform had been erected, presumably as they swam, because Roxie hadn't notice it before. Katie was on the platform in front of a microphone stand, holding a champagne flute and a spoon that she was tapping against the glass.

'Thank you!' She smiled at the crowd and held up a hand. 'I promise I won't take up much of your time. I'm delighted to see you enjoying yourselves. I just wanted to thank you all for coming today and supporting the grand opening of the refurbished Wisteria Hollow Lido. It started as a dream, became a plan and,' she laughed, 'a bit of an obsession. And now… it's ready for you all to enjoy.'

Cheers and applause came from the crowd.

'We are lucky enough to have local celebrity Stuart Philpot to officially open the lido today, so while he makes his way to the stage, could you all grab a drink? There's juice or champagne, whatever you fancy, and please excuse the paper cups but they're made from recycled paper that can be recycled again, as part of our efforts to avoid plastic wherever possible.'

As if by magic, waiting staff appeared carrying trays of juice and bubbly. Roxie and Lila accepted cups of champagne.

'Delicious.' Roxie raised the cup to Lila.

'She hasn't scrimped on anything today,' Lila said licking her lips.

'This is clearly important to her.'

Roxie looked over at Katie who was talking to Stuart, an easy smile on her face. Katie had goals, she became enthusiastic about things and she went after what she wanted. Roxie thought about herself and her life, about how she'd put everything into being a good wife, a homemaker and had enjoyed doing so. That had been enough for her, but now, looking at Fletcher and how things had worked out for them, was it enough going forwards? If he did leave her, what would she have left? She had interests and hobbies, but she had focused on him and his career, on making him happy and trying to heal from their loss. Or had she been trying to forget? No… she had never been able to forget, but she had tried to occupy herself with other things so that she didn't spend all her time grieving for the tiny duo that she'd never held, never nursed, never rocked to sleep, but had always loved.

Stuart tapped the microphone on the stand and quiet fell over the lido again.

'Hello!' He grinned and waved. 'It's great to be here today and I'm honoured to be asked to do this. Thank you, Katie.' He flashed her a smile and Katie's cheeks coloured slightly. It could have been the heat, or it could have been because Stuart was, Roxie supposed looking at him now, a fairly attractive man. *If you like that sort of thing…*

'We decided not to do a traditional ribbon cutting but Stuart suggested he could start the celebrations by taking a swim.'

'Feel free to take photographs.' Stuart beamed at everyone, puffing out his chest like a bird, and Lila sniggered.

Roxie patted her friend's knee. 'Behave.'

'I know, but really? He's after some free promo.'

'He's not hurting anyone.'

'I guess you're right, it's just that I'm certain that if he was chocolate he'd eat himself.'

Whistles pierced the air as Stuart removed his shirt, exposing a tanned muscular body. He was already wearing colourful swimming shorts, but he kicked off his flip-flops and strutted to the edge of the pool.

Posing there for a moment while people took photos on their mobile phones, he flexed his biceps and grinned at them, flashing bright white teeth that contrasted so well with his (possibly fake) tan. As he turned from side to side, his abdominals rippled and a few cheers came from the crowd, making his grin widen.

'I am beyond delighted to now declare the lido… officially OPEN!'

He raised his arms above his head then bounced off his toes and dived gracefully into the water. Cheers filled the air and Katie clapped her hands from the platform.

'Thank you so much, Stuart!' she shouted above the noise. 'Have a great day, everyone!'

Roxie sat back and sipped her drink as Stuart did a few lengths of the pool, pausing at each end for photographs. She wondered what hashtags they would acquire, and if the exposure would bring more people to the village and to the lido. It was set to be a long, hot summer, and what was better than spending it outdoors with access to cool, clear water and a variety of mocktails?

~

'This looks pretty special, Glenda,' Fletcher said as they walked into the lido grounds. He had paid at the gate, not having purchased a ticket previously. Roxie had bought two and asked if he wanted to go but that was weeks ago, possibly months, and at the time he recalled being a bit dismissive.

That thought stung. How many times had he seemed disinterested in things that Roxie wanted to do? How often had he been so tired and worn down by the week that he'd ignored her suggestions or plans and made her feel insignificant? Come to think of it, over recent months Roxie's efforts at getting him to plan something with her for the weekends had diminished, practically stopped altogether. Had his indifference widened the gap between them?

He felt himself weakening, and wished he'd stayed home, that he was lying on the sofa or even in bed. Exhaustion was blurring his edges and wearing him down. Sleep would be good right now; sleep was an escape from stress and anxiety. BUT… He wanted to make things better, to try to fix his marriage. He would do everything in his power to make things better.

Glenda trotted along in front of him, her head turning from side to side as she took in the sights. Whenever she spotted another dog, she gave an excited bark, and Fletcher knew she wished she could be off the lead, running around with her canine friends. But, of course, if dogs were allowed off lead, it would lead to chaos and would also be unfair on those members of the public who were not dog lovers.

When the pool came into view, Fletcher could see people standing around taking photographs. He walked closer and peered over someone's shoulder. There, in the pool, was Stuart Philpot, local bodybuilder and expert poser. Fletcher chuckled to himself. Stuart was a pleasant enough guy, but he certainly showed some signs of being a narcissist. That didn't seem to be deterring his fan base though as they called to him to smile in their direction while they snapped away on their mobile phones. Off to the far side of the pool, there was a professional photographer, presumably from the local press, no doubt there as part of the publicity for the opening of the lido.

'Come on Glenda, let's look for Mum, shall we?'

He turned and scanned the sunloungers, his gaze falling on sunbathers, parents and children, couples and groups of friends.

Then he spotted her, and his breath caught in his throat.

Roxie... Wow!

She was standing between two sunloungers, peering over the top of huge sunglasses at someone with blonde hair. *Lila! She was, of course, with Lila.* His eyes were drawn straight back to his wife though, because she looked incredible in a sexy black swimming costume that showed off her gorgeous body to perfection.

The emotions that coursed through him battled for prime position: love, pride, desire, vulnerability. There she was, toned and smooth-skinned, wearing very little in a public place. Other people were in swimwear too, but Fletcher didn't even see them; he saw only his wife. He was torn between wanting to gaze at her all afternoon and wishing he could throw a towel over her so that no one else could see her beauty. His hand strayed self-consciously to his belly, the evidence of his own indulgence and lack of exercise.

As if sensing his gaze upon her, she turned her head and looked right at him. He raised a hand, his mouth opening as if to say hello, but she just stared as if looking right through him.

What was wrong? Did she hate him? Had he hurt her so badly she'd never forgive him?

When she turned back to Lila then sat down, without acknowledging him, he realised what had happened. She wasn't wearing her prescription sunglasses, so she probably hadn't even seen him.

'Come on, Glenda.'

He led the dog through the crowd, past the rows of sunloungers and umbrellas until he reached Roxie and Lila.

'Afternoon, ladies,' he said.

Roxie stood up, clearly surprised to see him, and he pressed a gentle kiss to her cheek. She smelt of coconut sun cream, her familiar sweet perfume and fresh cut limes. His heart thudded behind his ribs as he looked at her closely, taking in the curve of her slim hips, the swell of her breasts and the hollow at the base of her throat. It had been a while since Fletcher had felt such strong desire. He had always wanted Roxie, always adored her, but didn't often feel this depth of longing anymore. Yet here, today, he wanted to pick her up and carry her home then show her exactly how much he still loved and wanted her.

'Hi Fletcher.' Lila smiled then stood up. 'I was just off to the bar to get more drinks. Would you like one?'

'Uh... yes please. A lemonade or something soft would be great, thanks.'

'No problem. Same again, Roxie?' Lila asked.

'Yes please, Lila.'

When they were alone, Roxie whispered, 'Why are you looking at me like that?'

'You look incredible, Rox.' He reached out and gently brushed the back of his fingers against her cheek and her pupils dilated, showing him that she felt it too, that their connection wasn't completely gone, that something still burned between them.

'Thank you. It's... nice that you think so.' She leant forwards and rubbed Glenda's head. 'What are you doing here? I thought you didn't want to come.'

'I'm sorry about that. I should have made more of an effort. I feel terrible. I... brought Glenda and I hoped we could spend some time together.'

Roxie pressed her lips together then sighed slowly.

'Oh Fletcher... What a mess.'

'Don't say that. We can fix this, Rox, I know we can.'

Roxie opened her mouth as if to reply but cheering from over by the raised platform stopped her.

'What's going on?' Fletcher asked.

A man wearing a Hawaiian shirt and bright red swimming shorts was standing on the platform waving his hands at everyone.

'Thank you! Thank you! So sorry to disturb your day, but, uh… I need to do something and I'd appreciate your support.' He blew out his cheeks then cleared his throat. 'I hope this is okay with you all. I did ask Katie's permission.' He looked around and spotted Katie standing with Stuart Philpot and the press photographer. Stuart had a towel draped around his shoulders and Katie was smiling up at him. She seemed to realise her attention was required so she gave the man on the platform a double thumbs up. 'Thanks, Katie.'

Fletcher didn't recognise the young man, who looked around mid twenties, but that didn't mean he wasn't local.

'Okay… okay… this is… right.' He pushed a shaky hand nervously through his thick blond hair. 'My name is Henry Crook. I'm not from Wisteria Hollow but my girlfriend is. Hattie, would you come up here for a moment, please?'

All heads turned as a young woman in a green bikini made her way through the sunloungers, her cheeks flaming red, her eyes fixed on Henry.

'This amazing woman is my best friend, my lover, my soul-mate. She has been everything to me since we first met, and I can't imagine life without her. I want to give her everything, to make her life as incredible as I can. See… when we met at university in Bristol, I was studying law and she was studying English literature. We became friends, then more than friends, but at the end of my third year, I became ill. I ignored it for a while, hoping my health would improve but it didn't, and Hattie insisted I go to the doctor. I… was tested and, luckily for me, I now believe, it turned out to be coeliac disease. I thought it was something worse, was worried that it could be something dreadful that would kill me, but it turned out to be a gluten allergy. As soon as I made changes to my diet, I started to feel better and now, as long as I avoid gluten, I don't have any problems. But even when I was terrified that it could be something much worse, Hattie was there by my side, supporting me, reassuring me and loving me. She would have held my hand to the…' His voice broke and he lowered his head and rubbed at his eyes. When he looked up again, everyone in the lido grounds was silent, waiting for him to finish. 'I was going to say that she would have held my hand to the end. See… we all feel lonely at times and I have felt the darkness that comes with feeling isolated and lonely. Sadly, I think most people have. But since I met Hattie, that darkness has been banished by her sunshine.' He smiled then and held out his hand as Hattie stepped up next to him. 'Today, I am lucky and I know exactly how lucky I am. My health is good and I have this wonderful woman in my life.'

He took her hand and kissed it and there was a collective intake of breath from the crowd.

'Hattie… my sunshine…' Henry went down on one knee and produced a small black box. 'Today, I would like to ask if you will do me the very great honour of being my wife.' He opened the box and a diamond ring glinted in the sunlight.

Hattie stood there for a moment, her brown hair falling around her face and her whole body trembling. Then she went down on her knees, so she was eye to eye with Henry.

'I will, Henry, I will.'

Henry placed the ring on her finger then they stood up and he pulled her into his arms. As they kissed, everyone clapped and cheered, and Fletcher had a lump in his throat. It wasn't every day that he witnessed such an honest outpouring of love and gratitude and it was so close to home right now. Such a reminder of his own situation and of how he and Roxie had started out, how devoted and intense their love had been in the early days. The couple now completely lost in each other on the platform weren't any different to how he had Roxie had been. Love was love and it grew from a spark that could continue to burn brightly as long as it was tended.

Fletcher turned to Roxie and took her hand. At first, she was tense, but then she curled her fingers round his and let him pull her close.

'I know we have things to discuss, Rox, things to work through, but I love you, angel. I always have done, and I always will.'

She exhaled against his chest then raised her head and met his gaze.

'I love you too, Fletcher.'

When their lips met, everything around them disappeared and for a few precious moments, Fletcher felt that nothing else mattered at all.

The first proposal he'd made to Roxie all those years ago had been accepted. What was to stop him trying again?

7

'Roxie, angel? You awake yet? I'm going to take Glenda for a walk.'

Fletcher set a cup of tea on Roxie's bedside table then pressed a gentle kiss to her forehead, breathing in her scent; expensive moisturiser and beneath it, the natural fragrance of her skin, sweet and floral, familiar and rousing. She stirred then opened her eyes.

'Pardon?'

'I said I'm going to walk Glenda.'

'What time is it?'

'Just after eight.'

She sat up and rubbed her eyes. 'Why are you going so early?'

'I was up and about so I thought I'd make the most of the beautiful morning air.'

'Oh… okay.' A tiny line appeared between her brows.

Fletcher had hoped she wouldn't wake-up properly because he hated fibbing to her – and this was a fib, not a lie, because it was for a good reason, and, besides, he did actually fancy a walk in the fresh air. Plus, of course, he wanted to do something nice for his wife, but he wanted it to be a surprise. Now though, as Roxie was awake, he worried that she'd hear the wobble in his tone or see the worry in his eyes, so he looked away and went to the window instead, peering at the back garden through the gap in the curtains. He opened the window and let the sweet air into the room, hoping it would distract Roxie.

'I won't be long. Is there anything special you fancy for breakfast?'

'I'm too sleepy to think right now.'

'Shall I surprise you?'

'That would be nice, thanks.' She smiled and he smiled back.

Gazing at her now, with her sleep-mussed hair and smooth skin, her strappy nightdress clinging to her curves and the bed still warm, it took all his strength not to jump back under the covers and pull her into his arms. But that wouldn't be right, not yet. They had enjoyed a relaxing evening together after their return from the lido, the kiss they had shared following the young couple's poolside proposal uniting them in a way they hadn't been in some time. However, when they got home, they were cautious around each other, careful of disturbing the fragile status quo. There were matters they needed to discuss, things they needed to air, but the timing had to be right. And so, they had opened a bottle of red wine, sat in the garden and drunk it as twilight fell and the air was laced with the scents of honeysuckle and roses, as the stars popped out in the sky and Glenda had fallen asleep on Roxie's lap like a baby. Then they'd gone inside, eaten a light supper and headed to bed where they'd cuddled, Roxie's head on his chest, arm flung across his stomach and his face pressed into her hair. They had been loving but almost shy with each other, hesitant to do more than cuddle in case they broke the spell and unsettled each other again.

'Right… okay then… I'll see you in a bit.' He raised his hand in a small wave then turned and left the bedroom. Glenda trotted along at his heels, keen to make the most of the offer of early exercise from one of her humans.

⁓

Roxie waited until she heard the front door closing then she slumped against the headboard. What *was* going on?

Yesterday, she and Fletcher had kissed in a way they hadn't done in as long as she could remember. She had felt his passion, his love and his commitment in that kiss and for a few precious moments she had felt secure in his love again. They'd come home, he'd suggested opening a nice bottle of wine and they'd relaxed in the garden, chatting about innocuous topics like people they'd seen at the lido, Lila and Ethan, whether they should buy more bedding plants and about the summer forecast.

She had wondered if, when they went to bed, Fletcher would kiss her again, if he would take her in his arms and make love to her in the way he used to do. Instead, he had cuddled her, holding her against his chest and she had fallen asleep like that, listening to the regular beat of his heart. It had been extremely comforting, and she had slept well, though when she had woken to find him already up and dressed, a flicker of sadness had darted through her. She had almost reached out a hand and asked him to come back to bed, but the worry that perhaps he wouldn't want to hold her and make love to her prevented her from doing so. Rejection would be too much to bear. She wanted him to desire her, but for now, she would be content with feeling that he loved her and cared for her, that he was happy to hold her close. That was precious. He was precious. She could still smell him on her skin, feel his imprint in the bed next to her, see the impression of his head upon his pillow.

She loved him so much still.

Why was he going out so early? Walking the dog was a perfectly feasible reason for leaving so early on a Sunday and yet, it was unusual for Fletcher, and Roxie was currently attuned to unusual behaviour. It was a sign of something, but whether it was good or bad she couldn't be certain. Was Fletcher actually off to walk the dog or was he up to something else?

It didn't have to be a bad something, and Roxie knew that she would normally think the best of her husband and not the worst, but with the way things had been recently, and following the attention he had received from Cynthia, Roxie was, she realised, on high alert.

And she did not like it, not one bit.

It just wasn't who they were; they had always been so close and in love, so certain of their partnership. Roxie had always been sure that they would spend their lives together, that when Fletcher retired, they would travel the world, do all the things they'd dreamt of doing when they first got together but hadn't found the time to do yet. Losing Fletcher wouldn't just mean losing him and their marriage, it would be losing the dreams they had shared, the plans they had made and their whole future. Marriage was about so much more than loving someone, it was a full-on commitment that had to be entered into wholeheartedly and Roxie had done exactly that.

The question was… Had Fletcher? And even if he had done so all those years ago, did he still stand by his vows?

Fletcher had walked Glenda around the block twice and hoped that it would ease his nerves but as he approached Lila's cottage again, his stomach rolled over. He knew Lila quite well and liked her, she was a kind woman who clearly cared about Roxie, but she was, essentially, Roxie's friend, not Fletcher's. How she would feel about what Fletcher was about to ask her, he had no idea.

It was now or never though, so he'd better get it done…

He knocked on the door, hoping that Lila wasn't a fan of a long Sunday lie in. If she was, he'd have to come back later, and he didn't fancy having to find another excuse to get away from Roxie.

The door opened and Lila stood there in denim dungarees and flip-flops, her blonde hair held back from her face with a red scarf. Her eyes widened when she saw Fletcher and heat filled his cheeks as his heart began to thud.

'Hello Fletcher. Everything okay?' Lila peered around him as if looking for Roxie.

'Uh... yes, yes... everything's fine, thanks.' He smiled but his lips twitched, and his neck stiffened, the tendons feeling so brittle they would snap if he so much as tried to turn his head.

'Roxie not with you?' she asked.

'She's still in bed.'

'Oh... right.' Lila smiled but there was uncertainty in her eyes.

'Sorry to call so early on a Sunday but I have a favour to ask and I needed to speak to you when Roxie wasn't around.'

'Okay. Would you like to come in?' Lila gestured at the hallway.

'If that's all right?'

'Of course.'

Fletcher followed Lila inside, casting a glance behind him as if worried that their neighbours might see him going into Lila's house alone and wonder what was going on. The last thing he needed was for Roxie to suspect him of carrying on with Lila, but then would Roxie ever think that of her husband and her best friend? He was getting paranoid now, his mind working overtime; his fear of Roxie being hurt consuming him and blurring his common sense.

In the lounge, Fletcher looked around. He'd been here before when he'd popped in with Roxie and once, a long time ago, for dinner with Lila and *Ben the Bastard*, to give Ben the full epithet that Roxie had assigned to him, but he'd never visited without his wife; he hadn't had a reason to come here.

'Ethan not up?' he asked, looking around as if expecting to see the younger man.

'No… we um… he uh…' Lila's cheeks coloured. 'He hasn't stayed over yet. We're not rushing our relationship.'

'Oh!' Fletcher grimaced. 'I'm so sorry. I didn't want to assume anything. It's just that, obviously, I know you two are close and I assumed…' He smacked his forehead. 'What an idiot I am. Should never assume anything, of course I know that. But… I… uh …'

Stop talking, Fletcher!

'It's fine. Ethan and I are very fond of each other but we're taking things slowly.'

'Very wise.' Fletcher coughed self-consciously.

'Would you like a cup of tea or coffee?'

'That would be lovely, thank you, but I don't really have the time and if I go back smelling of coffee, Roxie will wonder where I've really been.'

'Is something wrong, Fletcher?' Lila narrowed her eyes and Fletcher felt something inside him shift, like sand on the shore being stirred by the waves and dragged back to the depths. He had a sudden urge to pour his heart out to Lila, to tell her how difficult things had been, how worried he was about Roxie and his relationship and how scared he was of losing her, but he knew that if he started down that path, he'd struggle to come back. So, instead, he swallowed hard, took a deep breath and smiled.

'Everything's… fine. Well, not exactly fine, as Roxie and I have been… experiencing a few difficulties. BUT!' He held up a finger. 'It will all be fine in the end, as they say.' He laughed but it sounded hollow.

'I don't know much about what's been going on, as Roxie tends to put on a brave face, but I did wonder if something was up. Roxie's wonderful at helping me with my life but not so good at asking for help. She has seemed a bit sad lately but whenever I try to speak to her about it, she changes the subject.'

'Sounds like Roxie.'

'What can I help you with then?' Lila tucked her hands into the pockets of her dungarees. 'I'll do anything I can to make things better for you and Roxie.'

'Okay… I know this will be hard for you because I'm going to ask you to keep a secret from Roxie, and she's your best friend, and she has an ability to sniff out a secret like a detective or the FBI, but this is for a very good reason.'

Lila chewed her bottom lip. 'I have to admit that the idea of keeping secrets does make me nervous. I don't like deceiving anyone, especially not those I love. But, I'm assuming there's a good reason for this?'

'There is.' He nodded. 'And I'm about to tell you why…'

~

'Where's Glenda?' Fletcher looked down at the lead he was holding. The harness at the end was empty and resting on the floor.

Lila gasped. 'I didn't notice her getting out of that.'

'Me either.' He looked around the lounge, but the small dog wasn't there. He hurried back to the hallway, but it was empty. He called up the stairs and listened, but no pattering of tiny paws informed him of her whereabouts. He'd been so engrossed in telling Lila about his plans that he hadn't even felt the dog tugging at the harness. Horror filled him as it dawned on him that he probably hadn't fastened it properly in the first place in his eagerness to leave the house that morning. If anything happened to Glenda, Roxie would never forgive him.

Back in the lounge, he held up his empty hands to Lila, so she turned and went through to the kitchen and Fletcher followed.

Glenda wasn't in there either.

A funny sensation fluttered in his chest and spread through him like an icy chill. He hadn't opened the front door since he got there so she couldn't have gone out that way and onto the road. She might be upstairs asleep or perhaps she'd climbed into one of Lila's cupboards and got stuck; she'd done that before in her own home and had to be rescued, but not for some time, not since she was a pup, and she was a loyal little thing; she preferred to be with her humans than on her own. So... something must have caught her attention.

'Where are your cats, Lila?' he asked, and Lila's eyes widened.

'Cleocatra is probably upstairs on one of the beds but William Shakespaw tends to spend more time in the garden. Although, since I've stopped my nightly shows, he does stay in more than before.'

'Nightly shows?' Fletcher wasn't aware of Roxie mentioning that Lila had been involved in any local amateur dramatics.

'Yes.' Lila's ears turned red and she adjusted the scarf holding her hair back. 'I spent quite a few nights wearing my wedding dress and singing karaoke after Ben left. It was my way of coping... with the loneliness and the way it seemed so empty here.'

'Ah... I think I recall Roxie mentioning something about that.' He gave her shoulder a gentle pat. 'Difficult time.'

'It was, but we all have our ways of coping and that was mine. Once I got rid of the dress and the accessories, it really helped.'

'I'm glad to hear it.' Fletcher wondered how he would ever cope if Roxie left him. Their home would be so empty, so lonely, so... not a home. Home was where Roxie was, and if she wasn't there, it would be no more than an empty shell. 'And now you have Ethan.'

'He's lovely.' Lila's eyes took on a shine, as if the thought of Ethan carried her far away from the here and now. 'He's such a kind man and so... well...' She smiled and her cheeks turned pink.

'You're very fond of him.'

'Yes.'

A bark from outside made Fletcher jump. He'd momentarily been sidetracked by his thoughts about Roxie and fear of losing her, but he had to find Glenda and fast.

'The back garden!' Lila rushed to the door.

'How did she get out?' Fletcher followed her as she tugged on the door and hurried into the garden.

'The cat flap!'

Outside, Lila stopped so suddenly that Fletcher almost collided with her and he had to put out his hands to find his balance. He rocked on his heels and took a step backwards then another to stop himself from falling.

'Look!'

Lila pointed at the corner of the garden where a large black and white cat was staring into a lavender bush, its tail flicking from side to side, its fur standing on end like an upturned brush. The cat was making a strange strangled sound, something between a meow and a growl, and it made Fletcher shudder.

'It's like something out of a horror movie.'

Lila gave a wry laugh. 'You should hear it in the middle of the night when he's having a go at other cats. Terrifying.'

Lila approached the cat then crouched down next to it. 'Come on now, Willy. That's just Glenda. No need to be so aggressive. She won't hurt you.' Her voice was soft, her tone soothing as if speaking to a frightened child.

Fletcher crouched next to Lila and peered into the bush. 'Oh Glenda.' Pressed into the lavender, so that it seemed to sprout out around her like some sort of Elizabethan ruff, was the tiny pug, her eyes bulging, her whole body trembling. He shuffled towards her on his knees and reached for her then brought her to his chest. 'Did the scary cat frighten you, sweetheart?'

Glenda remained silent, trembling violently in his arms, so he stood up slowly and hugged her to him, stroking her soft head.

'You are a bully, Willy. Do you hear that?' Lila shook her head at the cat as she stood up. As if completely unaware of what he'd done, Willy started to wind himself around Lila's legs. 'I am so sorry. Poor Glenda.' Lila reached out and stroked the small dog. 'She must have seen him coming out and followed him, then he turned on her. He's very territorial.'

'Glenda would just have wanted to play. She's a sweet little thing.'

'I know she is. I'm sorry, Glenda, for my cat's antisocial behaviour.'

'She'll be fine, but I'd better get her home.' Fletcher turned and went through the cottage to the front door where he put Glenda's harness back on and double-checked that he'd fastened it securely. 'So, you're all right about keeping what we discussed to yourself?'

'Absolutely.' Lila flashed him a smile. 'It will be just wonderful.'

'I hope so.'

Outside on the street, he set Glenda down and they made their way home, Fletcher feeling a renewed sense of hope that telling Lila about his plans would help them come to fruition.

8

Outside her parents' home, Roxie parked the car and cut the engine. As soon as the air conditioning stopped, the car started to warm up. It was only eleven a.m. but the day was sunny, and the forecast had predicted a hot afternoon. At least the barn conversion her parents lived in on the edge of a working farm was large and cool with plenty of surrounding trees to offer shelter.

She opened the door and got out then stretched her legs. The journey had only taken forty-five minutes, but her legs were already stiff, probably because she'd been stuck behind a tractor for the last two miles of country lanes, so there had been a lot of stopping and starting to pull in and allow oncoming traffic to pass. Driving through narrow country lanes wasn't her favourite pastime but it was the only way to get to her parents' home and therefore a necessity.

The barn had belonged to a small farm that had been amalgamated with the neighbouring one many years before, when the children of the farmers had fallen in love. When they married, they had joined their land, but sold a small section of the one farm to Roxie's parents, along with the barn that they had subsequently converted. Her parents were both keen gardeners and their very large back garden had a section devoted to vegetables, herbs and fruit, and whenever Roxie visited, she always went home with plenty of organic produce. The setting was such a beautiful green space with a variety of trees and hedgerows edging the property, fields stretching into the distance bright with the lemon of rapeseed, the pale violet of borage and the yellow and brown of sunflowers. Roxie imagined that if she viewed the area from above it would resemble a patchwork quilt.

She went around to the back door of the car, opened it, then undid the special clip that fastened to Glenda's harness. Glenda licked her hand and Roxie pressed a kiss to her head.

'Good girl. Time to see Nanna and Bampa?'

Glenda barked with excitement. She loved coming to see Roxie's parents because they doted on her like she was a grandchild. Which she was, really, because they didn't have any human grandchildren. Roxie had intended coming to see her parents the previous Sunday, following the opening of the lido, but she'd needed some time to gather her thoughts after Cynthia had answered Fletcher's phone. She'd wanted to ensure that she could maintain her composure around her parents. Her mum would be able to tell if Roxie was upset and she didn't want to have to explain what had happened to them. So now it was Thursday, almost a week to the day, and she thought (hoped) she was a lot calmer.

Roxie set Glenda down and the dog ran to the front door where she waited on the mat, her tiny tail waggling. Roxie retrieved the bunch of pink tulips from the boot and the bottle of craft gin, then locked the car and went to the front door.

She rang the bell and waited, even though she knew the door would be unlocked. Her parents were terrible with security, believing that because they lived out in the countryside, no one would try to break in, and Roxie felt compelled to remind them of the risks every time she visited. Being born right at the end of the Second World War meant that her parents believed that because they'd survived that, nothing else could harm them. Her father, a wiry man of seventy-six, often spoke about how he could take down any of the youth of today who dared come near him or his home, and so far, nothing Roxie or Fletcher had said to the contrary had convinced him otherwise.

Footsteps sounded in the hallway then the door swung open and her mother stood there, clad in her usual floral dress and sandals with a low heel. Her ash blonde hair was fashioned into Marilyn Monroe style soft waves, a dusting of powder on her face with a dash of blusher and her trademark pale pink lipstick. Lucy Smith was an attractive seventy-five-year-old woman who looked a good ten years younger, and she hadn't changed at all for as long as Roxie could remember. Her hair and clothing were the same style as they'd always been; it was possible that some of them were the same vintage items from Roxie's childhood. Perhaps though, she thought, as she looked at her mother now, she had filled out a little more around the hips and bust, her waist thickened a touch, her cheeks slightly plumper, but she was still beautiful, still Roxie's mum.

'Hello, my darling.' Lucy opened her arms and Roxie stepped into her hug, her mum's soft curves comforting and familiar, her perfume a mixture of baking and oranges. 'It's so good to see you.'

'Good to be here, Mum.'

And just like that, tears sprang into her eyes. She looked down at the flowers in her arms to gain a moment to compose herself.

'These are for you. A little crushed now after that hug, but they'll come back to life if you get them in some water.'

'They're beautiful, Roxie, my favourite colour.'

'I know.' Roxie smiled. 'And I got Dad a bottle of that gin he was on about last time I was here. There were so many on that craft gin website that I couldn't remember what flavour he wanted, so I went with the lemon one. Is that okay?'

'Of course, it is! You know how much he loves gin and tonic.' Her mother was already leaning over and patting Glenda's head. 'And how's my favourite little girl?'

'She's good. Aren't you, Glenda?'

Glenda barked, making them both laugh.

'Come on then, let's get the kettle on.'

Her mum bustled into the large cool hallway with Glenda right behind her, so Roxie followed, seizing the opportunity to wipe at her eyes with the back of her hand. It was silly getting so emotional, but she hadn't seen her mum for a few weeks and the hug had brought everything right to the surface like bubbles in a fizzy drink.

'Dad's in the garden, of course, so if we make tea, we can take it out and enjoy it in the sunshine. We've been having such lovely weather lately, haven't we? So delightful… and it's just perfect for the garden and the vegetables… but we've been a bit worried that we might have a drought later on this summer, though if we do… we have water saved in the barrels that your father has attached to every available drainpipe around the property.'

Roxie smiled as her mum chattered on, barely pausing to think, aware that this was her time to completely relax. Her mum could conduct an hour-long monologue and Roxie would only need to listen and nod. It was how her father coped too with Lucy's need to keep talking – to fill all rooms with her thoughts and feelings, her knowledge and her musings, as if silence was far too heavy to bear – he listened and nodded and only responded when prompted. There was something incredibly comforting about not having to make an effort, about just existing, and Roxie was glad to be there.

When the tea was made, they took it out to the garden. While her mum laid it out on the table, Roxie walked along the path to the vegetable patch where her father was on his knees on a gardener's mat, his bare hands covered in soil, his head protected by the cowboy hat that he'd bought years ago on a trip to America. He loved that hat and had worn it for as long as Roxie could remember, telling her when she was younger that he had once been a cowboy who'd herded cattle and ridden with outlaws. Roxie had loved the stories he'd told her about his time sleeping on a bedroll under the stars and eating beans out of a tin as he sat around a campfire with his companions. Of course, none of it was true, and some of it was probably based on movies he'd seen, but it made for good bedtime stories and gave him an exciting air of adventure. When she'd asked where her mum had been during all of this, he'd told her that she'd been right there beside him, wearing her own boots and chaps, that she'd been a better rider that all of the men and that she could tame a wild horse with a smile and an apple. That had made Lucy chuckle and swat her husband's arm playfully, which always led to her parents gazing adoringly at each other as if seeing each other for the first time all over again. It had sparked Roxie's own longing to find a man who would be her other half, the cowboy of her own adventure. To have a man look at her in the way that her dad looked at her mum would be very special indeed, and then, one day, she'd found that in Fletcher.

For a long time, she'd had that security, believing that no one could tear her and her husband apart, only now it seemed that someone else was looking at him that way too.

Roxie shook herself. No sense dwelling on that right now, especially not when Fletcher was in work miles away and she had come to visit her parents. The last thing they deserved was to have their daughter visiting in a state of melancholy, to have her drop the bombshell that she was worried her husband might be having an affair when it was probably the furthest thing from the truth. Amazing how quickly belief in a relationship could be turned around, how something so solid could crumble so quickly.

'Hi Dad.'

He turned and smiled, his eyes shaded by his hat so she could only see his patchy white stubble and the rosy tip of his nose.

'Well hello there, Roxie.'

He dusted his hands on his jeans, but Roxie could see that they were still caked with mud, then stood up. His work uniform of jeans with braces and an old striped shirt made her smile. The waist of the jeans was far too loose, hence the braces, but he refused to throw anything out, even though he'd lost weight in the past two years leaving a lot of his clothes at least a size too big.

'Aren't you a sight for sore eyes?

'Sorry?' She gently pushed his hat back on his head and met his gaze. 'Your eyes are sore? Are they playing up again?'

'No, no!' He waved a hand. 'They've been fine since I got those new reading glasses. I just meant that it's good to see you. You're looking wonderful as always, just like your mum.'

He pulled her into a hug then released her. 'Whoops! Got mud on that lovely shirt.'

Roxie looked down, and sure enough, her dad's muddy fingerprints decorated the sleeves of her lilac linen blouse. 'It's okay, it'll wash.'

'I hope so. Your mother's forever reprimanding me for getting mud on her clothes. I tell her she's lucky I still want to keep grabbing hold of her all the time.' He laughed then winked at Roxie.

'She is lucky, Dad.'

'And so am I!' He rubbed his hands together. 'A very lucky man.'

'We've made tea.' Roxie gestured at the house where her mum was now sitting under the sun umbrella with Glenda on her lap. She appeared to be feeding Glenda something from a saucer. 'And it looks like Mum is giving Glenda tea again.'

'She does like to spoil our grandchild.' He laughed and shook his head. 'Yes let's have a cuppa and a catch-up, shall we?'

They made their way back along the garden path and Roxie sat at the table while her dad went inside to wash his hands.

'It looks like you've got a lot of veg growing this year. More than last year, anyway?' she asked her mum. Lucy looked up from petting Glenda.

'Yes, we have. Your father sowed a variety of different seeds so there's plenty to eat, freeze and pickle.'

'Sounds fabulous.' Roxie absently brushed at her sleeves.

'Oh, he didn't get mud on you, did he?'

'It doesn't matter, Mum. It will wash off.'

'I do hope so, dear. He's ruined so many of my blouses and dresses with his muddy paws.'

Roxie snorted. 'Paws?'

'Well, yes. Those big old hands of his are always in the mud. What can you do? I was telling Fletcher just the other day that your dad had gone and ruined one of my pillowcases by wiping his hands on it after he mistook it for a towel.'

Roxie frowned. 'Fletcher?'

'Yes, Roxie.' Her mum blinked. 'Why?'

'You spoke to Fletcher the other day?'

Her mum's eyes widened, and she opened and closed her mouth a few times. In a nearby tree a thrush warbled and it was met by the eclectic song of a blackbird.

'What's this?' Her dad appeared and pulled out the chair next to Roxie.

'Mum was telling me she spoke to Fletcher the other day.' Roxie shrugged nonchalantly, not wanting her parents to think she found it strange.

'I was telling him about you ruining my pillowcase. You know, the one you pulled out of the ironing basket?' Lucy stared at her husband.

Roxie looked from her mum to her dad and back again. It was as if her mum was trying to communicate something to her dad with her eyes. Suddenly, her dad's eyes widened, and he nodded, as if he'd remembered something. It was a look of realisation.

'Oh, yes... that's right. Fletcher rang to ask about... the uh... the roses.'

'Roses?' Roxie stared hard at her dad.

'Yes. He wanted some advice about pruning.'

'Oh... right.' Roxie brushed at her sleeves again, but the mud was going nowhere. *I do most of the gardening and anyway, I'm pretty sure Fletcher knows enough about pruning. Something about this isn't quite right; someone isn't telling the whole truth.* 'Why wouldn't he ask me?'

'Oh... uh... I think you were out.' Her mum patted the table gently. 'Roxie, will you pour please because I don't want to disturb Glenda. She's already had her tea on her special saucer.'

'Yes, of course.'

Roxie's mum kept a saucer especially for Glenda even though she used mugs for tea. It was a very sweet thing to do and made Roxie wonder about what her mum would have done for actual grandchildren. They would probably have loved coming here to see their wonderful grandparents, especially seeing as how they would only have had Roxie's mum and dad. Fletcher had lost his parents within a year of each other when he was in his early twenties, and Roxie had always admired how well he coped without them. Her parents meant the world to her and she was very grateful to still have them around.

Roxie poured milk then tea into three mugs and tried not to frown. Something was going on and she hadn't the faintest idea what. It wasn't unheard of that Fletcher might phone her parents, but he usually left that to her and spoke to them when they visited, so why he would phone them to ask about pruning the roses she had no idea. It was all a bit strange and... she had a feeling that something was definitely being kept from her.

What if he had told them he was leaving her because he wanted them to protect and support her through a difficult time? What if he had asked them to help her because he was unwell, and things would be difficult?

What if... what if...

She handed her parents their mugs then sat back and peered up at them over hers. Neither of them looked particularly sad or worried. In fact, they appeared to be rather pleased with themselves, as if they knew something and were concealing it for a reason, and as if they thought they'd done a very good job of it. They seemed oblivious to the fact that Roxie had real suspicions here and the last thing she wanted to do was to burst their bubble. She loved them far too much for that. So rather than push the matter, she sipped her tea and chatted about the weather and their vegetables, about Glenda and the squirrels she liked to chase from the garden when they came after her bird feeders, and about Lila and how well she was getting on with Ethan. Her parents liked to hear about young people in love and about any gossip from Sunflower Street, so Roxie did her best to entertain them, while putting her own suspicions to one side.

For today at least.

'Don't forget to breathe, Douglas!' yoga instructor and personal trainer Finlay Bridgewater called from the front of the village hall. 'If you keep holding your breath like that, you'll pass out.'

Roxie exhaled slowly then turned her head. Lila was grinning at her and pointing at the mat to her right. Roxie peered around Lila and sniggered because their friend Joanne Baker was snoring on her mat again. Joanne worked long shifts at the local café and had told them that she'd been suffering with insomnia recently, so that combination plus one of Finlay's relaxing Saturday morning yoga classes had sent Joanne off to sleep.

'Every Saturday,' Lila whispered, and Roxie nodded. Then she yawned. She hadn't been sleeping well herself lately and it had left her feeling less than her best. Since she'd been to see her parents two days ago, she'd been unable to forget what they'd said about Fletcher phoning them. She had resisted asking her mum and dad about it again, but she was curious about why they hadn't elaborated about the conversation and why Fletcher hadn't mentioned it at all. More and more, she was starting to feel that she didn't really know her husband as well as she'd always thought she did, and it wasn't a feeling she liked at all.

'Lila,' she whispered as Finlay led them into the downward dog.

'What?' Lila craned her neck to look at her, her face red from the effort of holding her position.

'Do you think everything's all right with Fletcher?'

'What? Why?' Lila's arms started to shake and sweat dripped off her forehead and landed on her yoga mat.

'Well… I think he's hiding something from me.'

Lila yelped and fell sideways, landing on the floor with a thump.

'Lila!' Roxie twisted around and crawled to her friend's side. 'Are you okay?'

'Yes.' Lia winced. 'I just lost my balance.'

'You poor thing.' Roxie rubbed Lila's shoulder. 'Can you get up?'

She helped Lila to sit then Finlay came over to them and asked her to move her limbs and if her head hurt at all, but Lila insisted she hadn't bumped her head and that she was fine.

'I think you'd better sit quietly for the rest of the class,' Finlay said, his face etched with concern.

'She'll be fine. I'll sit with her,' Roxie said as she helped Lila to the back of the class where there was a row of chairs.

They sat quietly for a while, watching as the rest of the class continued, villagers they knew well bending, stretching and breathing deeply, sometimes farting with the effort of holding a certain pose. It was, Roxie realised, even quite relaxing to watch yoga, farting aside.

The hall smelt of old paint and wood, of books and chips, of feet and sweat. It was a funny combination but due to the fact that the hall was used for a variety of exercise classes, for the local book club, for playgroup and sometimes for other village events like cookery shows and jumble sales. It was as if the walls had absorbed everything over the years and no amount of cleaning or opening windows would ever expunge the aroma. It was, she realised, the aroma of community; of people coming together and learning, playing, laughing, dancing, singing and supporting one another. It was, quite simply, fabulous.

'Are you feeling better?' Roxie asked.

'I'm fine, honestly.' Lila smiled. 'I did just lose my balance.'

'Was it my question?' Roxie watched Lila's face carefully, her curiosity deepening as Lila avoided meeting her eyes, pulling at her yoga pants and letting the stretchy material snap back against her thighs.

'Oh... no... uh...' Lila looked up at the clock on the wall above the small stage. 'Is that really the time? Gosh... Roxie, I'm so sorry but I have to dash.'

'Gosh?' 'Dash?' Who was this woman?

'But we're meant to be going for breakfast at the café.' Lila stood up and Roxie did too as if they were joined together with an elastic band.

'Yes… but, I can't make it today. So sorry. Speak later.'

Lila pressed a kiss on Roxie's cheek then hurried from the hall, leaving Roxie even more confused than ever.

Fletcher had been behaving strangely.

Her mum and dad had behaved strangely.

And now her best friend was behaving strangely too.

Was it Roxie? Had she done something to repel them all? To annoy them? To offend them? Or was she being overly sensitive? She was sure it wasn't the latter because the people she knew and loved just didn't behave like this.

She walked around the edge of the hall, avoiding outstretched hands and fingers as she went, the members of the class now stretched out at the end of the session, some of them slipping into sleep. As she passed Finlay, she flashed him a smile and a small wave, then she turned, remembering Joanne, but she was still out cold, completely oblivious to everything that had happened. It was probably best to let her sleep while she could and she knew that Finlay would wake her at the end of the session.

As Roxie stepped out into the bright morning, she wished she could be a bit more like Joanne. Oblivion would be nice sometimes. Less worrying would be wonderful.

But then, that had never been how Roxie was and she doubted she would change now. However, she would like to know what was going on and hoped to find out soon.

9

The weekend had been quiet so far and Fletcher had left Roxie cooking Sunday lunch while he took Glenda for a walk. He had offered to help her, or to make lunch so she could relax and walk Glenda, but she had shaken her head and ushered him from the kitchen, telling him that she liked cooking.

Roxie had been quiet since she'd returned from visiting her parents a few days ago, and even quieter since her yoga class yesterday. He had asked if she was all right and she'd smiled, but the smile hadn't reached her eyes and he knew that something was wrong. Then he'd had a text from Lila yesterday evening to say that she was worried Roxie suspected something was going on. His mobile had been on the coffee table in the lounge as he and Roxie watched television, and when he'd seen the name on the display he'd almost choked on his wine.

Roxie had asked if he was all right and patted his back as if to help him clear his airways, but he'd reassured her that he was fine and had merely swallowed the wrong way. However, he'd seen the way she'd glanced at his mobile and worried she might think it was Cynthia again. He had even considered telling her everything right there and then, coming clean and getting it all out in the open, but doing that would have ruined the surprise and he so wanted for Roxie to feel special, to feel loved and cared about by her family and friends, but most of all by her husband.

If he could hold his nerve and just do this one thing, bring the plan to fruition, then he was sure it would be worth it. Although at this rate he was worried Roxie would be serving him with divorce papers before he got through the next two and half weeks.

He stopped walking for Glenda to sniff at a patch of grass and looked up, realising that he was in front of the small village church. The low stone wall was mossy and crumbling, it needed some care, attention and some money invested in it, but he knew that not many people attended the church these days. It still saw some weddings, with locals getting married there, and the odd christening, but over the years it had lost its purpose as a focal point of village life. More and more these days, people got married at country hotels, registry offices or on tropical beaches, and although the village of Wisteria Hollow still had a lovely warm community feel, things were changing all the time. Goodness knew what life there would be like in another twenty years, because so much could change in that time, after all, look at him and Roxie and what they'd been through. The only thing constant in life was change and sometimes that made him sad, but in some ways, it was a good thing. Life shouldn't remain stagnant, places should change, just like people. He believed that the village would always be home for him and Roxie, but they would need to move with the times, just like everyone else.

He gave a low whistle and Glenda looked up then they carried on walking, Fletcher enjoying being outside, appreciating the bright blue of the sky, the rainbow of flowers in pots, borders and hanging baskets and the sweet scent that filled the air. Birds were singing in the trees, somewhere nearby someone was playing a saxophone, and in a local field, a tractor was rumbling along. It was a lovely morning to be alive and Surrey was a beautiful place to live. Fletcher was a lucky man and the best thing of all was that he would pick up the Sunday papers then go home to his beautiful wife; later on they would eat a roast with all the trimmings then sit in the garden and drink wine. Yes, he was keeping a secret from Roxie now, even though he hadn't been when she'd thought he was hiding something. But this secret was special, it was for her, and he hoped it would make her happy.

'Come on then, Glenda, let's get the papers then go home and see Mum.'

Glenda's pink tongue slid out and licked her flat little nose, and Fletcher smiled at her, convinced that she was smiling her approval.

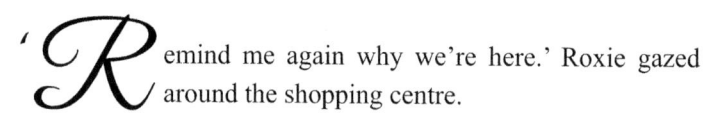

'Remind me again why we're here.' Roxie gazed around the shopping centre.

It was a large, sprawling rectangle built on the site of a former football stadium and made predominantly, it seemed to Roxie, of glass. Even though she was indoors, she was tempted to put her sunglasses on because the interior of the shopping centre was so bright.

'Well, I tried to find what I wanted locally and couldn't so I thought trying here would be a good idea because there are more shops, therefore a wider selection. Plus, it's only twenty-five minutes from home, so not far at all.' Lila grinned. 'Come on, it'll be fun.'

'You know me, Lila, I love to shop but I wasn't aware that you were a big fan.'

Lila shrugged. 'New man, new me.'

Roxie laughed. 'Ethan is such a positive influence on you, isn't he?'

'I like to look nice for him, it's true, but also for myself, and seeing as how he said he's going to take me out somewhere fancy, I thought I'd treat myself to a new dress.'

'You know what?'

'Tell me.'

'I might treat myself to something too.'

'I was hoping you'd say that, especially seeing as how we've bunked off yoga to come shopping.'

'I'm shocked that it's been two weeks since we last went. You're a bad influence on me, Lila, but you were right not to go last week after your little fall the previous Saturday and today… well… shopping wins.'

Lila hadn't really been hurt after she'd lost her balance but she'd said she wanted to be careful for a few weeks and Roxie had been tired and glad of the chance to take it easy last week and today the chance to go shopping appealed more than the idea of yoga.

They walked past shops selling sports gear, shoes, jewellery, electronics and mobile phones, then stopped outside a fancy looking boutique.

'Shall we take a look in here?' Lila asked.

The window display was a rainbow of summery dresses and sandals, culottes and frilly blouses; a variety of possibilities available inside.

'Yes, come on.' Roxie couldn't wait to take a look.

Lila went inside first, and Roxie followed. The shop smelt of leather, vanilla and furniture polish. Bright lights reflected in mirrors, on steel rails and on the counter off to the left. A shop assistant, wearing one of the floral tea dresses Roxie had seen in the window, with her black hair slicked back into a tight ponytail that left her forehead impossibly smooth, looked up from the garment she was folding as they entered and flashed them a smile. Roxie smiled back.

'What sort of dress were you thinking of getting?' she asked Lila.

'I'm not sure but I'm hoping I'll know when I see it.'

'With your colouring and lovely figure, you could go for anything.'

'You're so kind to me, Roxie.'

'I'm just being honest, sweetheart.'

They started browsing the rails, pausing now and then to hold up a dress to see what the other thought of it, and finally they had both selected five dresses.

'Let's do this, shall we?' Lila marched towards the counter. 'Can we try these on, please?'

'Of course.' The shop assistant smiled. 'The changing rooms are at the rear of the store. My colleague will help you should you require any assistance.'

Outside the changing rooms, another woman, who looked like a blonde version of the assistant at the counter – as if the shop was run by beautiful clones – directed them through an archway. There was a central space surrounded by six separate cubicles complete with heavy grey curtains on metal rails.

'Try one on then let me see,' Lila said.

'Deal!' Roxie scurried into one of the cubicles.

She drew the curtain across the rail then hung the dresses on the hooks on the wall and stripped to her underwear, trying not to look at her reflection. Changing room mirrors were never flattering, which was strange really, as surely they should be in order to persuade people to buy more? She removed one of the dresses from the hanger then slipped it over her head. The bright orange dress clung to her frame and made her skin look a strange shade of brown, as if she'd been dipped in a jar of coffee. She had spent more time outdoors over the past three weeks, what with a few trips to the lido and more time gardening, but she hadn't realised she'd tanned that much. Perhaps it was the dress and the harsh lighting in the changing rooms.

'Ready?' she called as she pushed back the heavy grey curtain.

'Ready!' Lila appeared in front of her.

'Wowzer…' Roxie gazed at her friend, admiring how the bright blue dress with its daisy print complimented her skin and brought out the colour of her eyes. 'That really suits you.' It had capped sleeves, a round neckline and it fell to Lila's knees.

'I do love the colour.'

'But is it fancy enough for a night out?' Roxie frowned.

'That's what I was wondering.' Lila pursed her lips.

'You could always get it anyway, for another time, and try one of the others for your night out.'

'Good idea.' Lila cocked her head on one side. 'Only… I don't want to hurt your feelings… but I'm not sure about that orange one, Roxie.'

'I know. It makes me look like I've been bronzed in gravy browning and shows off every lump and bump of my underwear, even though I'm wearing those *apparently* invisible panty line knickers.'

They giggled as Roxie pointed at the very visible VPL cutting the cheeks of her bottom in half.

'I seem to have four bum cheeks now.' Roxie shuddered. 'Ew!'

Desperate to stop seeing her reflection in the orange dress, Roxie hurried back to the cubicle to change. When they met again, they looked hard at each other.

'I like that one, Roxie.' Lila waved her hand in a circular motion. 'Turn around.'

Roxie did and Lila let out a low whistle. 'That is one *sexy* feminine dress.'

'But it's black.' Roxie wrinkled her nose. 'Not particularly summery or interesting.'

'I know, but… it's classy and it really suits you. It's the type of dress you can wear again and again.'

Roxie ran her hands down the silky material, feeling how it draped over her hips as if it had been made especially for her. The thin straps exposed her toned shoulders and arms and the hours of work she'd put in getting them that way, and the hem sat just above her knees. The neckline dipped just enough to expose a hint of cleavage and would be perfect with a plunge bra. She knew that Fletcher would love the dress. He had always loved her in black dresses, said it made him think of their early days together when she'd get dressed up to go on dates with him.

What woman wouldn't want to be desired by her partner? Why should Roxie be any different, especially in light of how things had been recently? If she could make Fletcher's pulse quicken, make him desire her again, then the dress would be worth the rather high price tag.

'I'll get it then.'

'Are you going to try the others on?'

'Yes, I will. But I think I know I'm going home with this one.'

'Okay well let's try them all on and hopefully I'll find the one I want, then we can go and get some lunch.'

'Wonderful!'

Roxie went back into the changing cubicle and pulled the curtain across, then stood in front of the mirror and examined her reflection. With a pair of heels and some silver jewellery, if she had her hair done and put some make-up on, she would feel good about herself again. It wasn't the dress, cosmetics, shoes, or any of that that really mattered though, and she was well aware of it. It was about her self-confidence, about her liking herself, and the majority of the time she was happy with who she was. Lately, it had been harder to find her self-belief, her sense of contentment, but everyone went through rough patches and it didn't mean that things couldn't get better, did it? So, if a lovely dress made her feel good, then it wouldn't hurt to buy it. When she'd wear it, she didn't know, but at least if it was in her wardrobe then she'd have the option to put it on and try to find what she seemed to have lost.

10

Fletcher looked around the kitchen, checking everything was ready, and his eyes landed on the calendar. He couldn't believe it was the end of June already, the month had flown past leaving him dazed, but his plans had come to fruition and today was the 29th, the day before his twenty-fifth wedding anniversary.

He'd had to tell a few fibs again to get Roxie out of the house and to account for himself being at home. He'd said he was working from home because of a train strike (not true) but he'd hoped she wouldn't look at the news, and that Lila would keep Roxie so busy she wouldn't have a chance to look at the internet. Lila had agreed to keep Roxie busy all day so Fletcher could get on with things unhindered. Ethan had been here all day, finishing off decorating and helping Fletcher with his plan, and the caterers had been and gone, leaving a wonderful feast for the party guests.

The kitchen table was laid with a variety of nibbles and non-perishables and the food that needed to be kept cool was in the fridge. The wine fridge was stocked with champagne and

Chablis, as well as a few bottles of rosé. There were bottles of red, along with a wide variety of drinks at the outside bar, which was set up in the marquee Fletcher had hired for the event. It had been a busy day getting it all ready but Lila had been wonderful, telling Roxie she needed her help with a project she was working on for her online business, and booking her and Roxie into the hair salon that afternoon. Ethan had also proved to be very helpful, and Fletcher was looking forward to relaxing and chatting to him later when everything was running (hopefully) smoothly.

Outside, the sun was low in the late afternoon sky and there was just a whisper of a breeze. The marquee took up most of the lawn and a few waiting staff scurried about preparing tables, hanging bunting and stocking the fridges in the bar with soft drinks and mixers. A DJ was setting up on the decking at the end of the garden under a small canopy and he gave Fletcher a thumbs up when he spotted him, letting him know that his soundchecks had gone well.

Ethan was perched on the low wall that divided the grass from the paved area right outside the house and Glenda was at his feet, her legs to one side as she gazed up at the decorator she'd taken a shine to.

'I think it's all ready to go,' Fletcher said to Ethan as he approached him.

'It looks wonderful. Roxie will be delighted.'

'I hope so.' Fletcher's stomach clenched. They'd been getting on better since that day at the lido but were still being cautious around each other, slightly reserved, as if afraid that one fast move could destroy the equanimity. They still needed to talk about things, but every time Fletcher had tried to discuss Cynthia and the fact that he was not at all interested and never would be, Roxie had seemed to close down, as if she couldn't even bear to think about such things. Seeing how it hurt her, he didn't push it, even though he knew they needed to clear the air if they were to move on together. Hopefully, the party would go some way towards reassuring her so she would be able to trust him again, to trust in how much he adored her and in their relationship.

'It will all be fine.' Ethan smiled, and Fletcher took comfort from his confidence.

'I'm going to take one last look around then hop in the shower before guests start arriving.'

'Good plan. Anything else you need me to do?'

'No, but you've been great, a fantastic help, actually. Thank you.'

'I'll pop home and change then bring Mum back with me.'

'Excellent! See you very soon.'

Fletcher saw Ethan out then walked around the garden one last time, admiring how good it all looked, hoping that Roxie would feel the same.

*

'I feel a bit… overdressed, Lila.' Roxie stared at her reflection in Lila's bedroom mirror. She was wearing the black dress she'd bought when they'd gone shopping along with a pair of high black wedges. She'd had her hair, nails and make-up done at the salon and looked as if she was about to walk the red carpet rather than go to the local pub. Her hair had been washed, blow-dried and curled, then pinned up on one side so that the rest cascaded over her left shoulder in ebony waves. Her green eyes sparkled with emerald eyeshadow, and black kohl pencil enhanced their almond shape and gave them a sultry, smoky appearance.

Lila stood behind her, smiling. 'You look incredible, Roxie.'

'Thank you. So do you.'

Roxie turned and admired Lila's bright blue dress with the daisy print. She'd bought a pair of gold gladiator sandals and they went perfectly with it. Lila's hair had been styled into soft beach waves and her blue eyes glittered with gold eyeshadow, her lashes long, thick and dark with mascara.

'Let's go downstairs and have a glass of something and raise a toast to ourselves, shall we?' Lila grabbed her bag from the bed.

'I think I'll need to drink a bottle to pluck up the courage to go to the pub like this. People will think we're mad.'

'Stop worrying, Roxie. You're the one who's always telling me to let my hair down.'

Roxie couldn't deny it, so she led the way downstairs to the kitchen. It was a hot afternoon, but the old cottage was cool inside because of the thick walls and small windows, and when Lila opened the back door, the heat swept in like a wave, making them both gasp. Lila opened the fridge door and stood in front of it fanning herself. Roxie stepped close to do the same.

Roxie got her phone out of her bag and peered at the weather app. 'Hottest day of the year so far, apparently.'

'Put that away!' Lila grabbed the phone from Roxie's hand and turned it off. 'You don't want to be reading the news or weather now, do you? This is our evening together; girls only, remember?'

Roxie frowned but nodded. 'But I should turn it on, just in case Fletcher calls. He's probably going mad working from home. I guess I could pop over there before we have a drink just to check he knows what to have for dinner and he can always order a takeaway.'

'No! Don't be daft! It's fine, he'll be fine. Afterall, Roxie, he is a grown man.'

Roxie's pulse increased. Lila wasn't usually this assertive, but she seemed intent on having Roxie all to herself. She hoped everything was all right with her friend and that things hadn't gone wrong with Ethan, because Lila definitely seemed tense, as if she was holding something back. Roxie would go along with Lila's wishes for now, because if her friend needed to talk then she wanted to be there for her. She took her mobile from Lila and dropped it into her bag then got two champagne flutes from the cupboard.

They sat outside, sipping ice-cold champagne, condensation forming on the crystal glass and dripping onto their hands. But Roxie didn't mind, it was such a beautiful day and she was glad to be with Lila. They'd invited Joanne too, but she'd been down for an evening shift at the café, so it had ended up being just the two of them.

'Shall we finish this then get going?' Lila asked as she drained her glass and reached for the bottle.

'Good plan. I just need to pop to the loo.'

Roxie got up and headed inside. When she came back to the kitchen, she remembered that Lila had turned her mobile off and she didn't like the idea of Fletcher – or her parents – being unable to contact her, so she opened her bag and pulled her mobile out. She turned it on then waited for a moment to check if she had any messages.

The mobile buzzed and Fletcher's name appeared on the screen.

Roxie,
Come home asap.
Nothing's wrong but I need to speak to you about something.
F xx

She read the message twice more and her belly lurched. Something had to be wrong for him to message her like that. She hurried outside to find Lila crouching down stroking William Shakespaw.

'Lila, I have to dash home a minute.'

'What? Why?' Standing up, Lila glanced at her watch and her eyebrows rose. 'Let's have one more drink first.'

'I can't. Fletcher sent me a text asking me to go back. It sounded urgent.'

She felt too warm, the silky dress was clinging to her skin and she was light-headed from the alcohol.

'Okay, well hold on a moment and I'll come with you.' Lila got up and grabbed the empty bottle and their glasses, both recently replenished.

'It's all right. I can come back for you after I've spoken to him.'

'Nope! I'm coming and that's that.'

Five minutes later, Lila had locked up the cottage and they were making their way along Sunflower Street to Roxie's home. Their shoes tapped on the hot pavement and dust rose into the air. Roxie's mouth was dry. She had to force herself not to run as worry scratched at her edges, telling her something was wrong because Fletcher was never one for being overly dramatic.

'Isn't it your anniversary tomorrow?' Lila asked as they walked.

Roxie swallowed hard. 'Yes.'

'Do you have anything planned?'

'Not really.'

And they didn't. She hadn't mentioned their impending anniversary because she'd been worried that Fletcher might have forgotten and she didn't want to put any pressure on him. Weeks ago, she'd ordered him a single malt that she knew he'd like, a silk tie and a new coffee machine, wrapped them and hidden them away, but she hadn't wanted him to feel he had to get her something. If he remembered, then it would be wonderful. If not, then she would deal with that herself, in her own way. It would hurt, of course it would, but it would also confirm some of her suspicions, and she would have to be strong.

'Oh, you should do something, Roxie.' Lila jogged along at her side and Roxie made an effort to slow her pace a bit.

As they neared her driveway, she frowned. There were several cars parked outside on the road, and the one belonged to her parents. What were they doing here?

Her heart dropped to her wedges. Was something wrong with her mum or dad? Did they have bad news?

She froze at the bottom of the drive, her breaths coming fast and shallow.

'Roxie, what's wrong?' Lila asked, placing a hand on Roxie's shoulder.

'Something is going on and I'm scared.'

Lila took Roxie's face gently in her hands and met her eyes.

'I promise you that nothing is wrong. Nothing at all. In fact, it's all very good. Stay calm, head on inside and you'll soon see.'

'Really?'

'One hundred percent.' Lila kissed her cheek. 'You're going to have a wonderful evening.'

Roxie turned back to her home, taking in how glorious it was with the large windows that let in so much natural light, the trees with their full branches and leaves offering shade and shelter, the flowers in the pots and borders, bright bursts of colour and scent.

Everything would be okay. Nothing was wrong. She had to believe it.

Lila took her hand and they walked up the driveway together.

∽

The guests were waiting in the marquee, including Roxie's parents, Roxie's friend Joanne, Ethan's mother Freda, Finlay the yoga instructor, and other friends from the village.

Fletcher kept dashing from the marquee to the kitchen to the hallway and back again. He was in knots now, hoping that Roxie would come home, hoping that she would be happy at the surprise.

Then he remembered he had one more job to do.

'Glenda?' He scanned the garden for the dog but there was no sign of her. She'd no doubt got caught up in the excitement and was probably with Roxie's mum and dad being spoilt. He'd have to go and find her though because she had an important role to play in proceedings.

~

Roxie slid her key into the lock but it wouldn't turn. She pulled it out, checked it was the right key, then tried again. Still nothing. She turned to Lila, unease tingling her fingers and toes and prickling her armpits.

'My key doesn't work.'

'Then knock.' Lila smiled, looking very pleased with herself.

Roxie turned back to the door and knocked, and it swung open.

'Good evening, ladies,' Ethan said as he grinned at them. 'Please do come inside.'

He stood back and they entered the hallway.

'Ethan? Are you still working?' Roxie frowned at him. 'You should go on home.'

'Everything's finished now,' he said. 'I ticked off all the jobs on my snag list and cleared away my tools. However, this evening I'm here to escort you to your husband.'

'What? Why?'

Roxie looked around her hallway, taking in the vases of fresh flowers, the fairy lights wound around the banister and the small candles creating a pathway along the floor that led through the hall and into the kitchen.

'Don't worry… the candles are battery powered, so there's no chance of Glenda knocking them over and setting the house on fire.' Ethan winked.

'Okay…' Roxie accepted his proffered arm and allowed him to lead her through to the kitchen.

The table was laid with a variety of canapés including garlic stuffed olives, goats cheese and asparagus tartlets, smoked salmon vol au vents and trays of sandwiches and mini rolls. Behind it stood two women wearing black trousers and white shirts with black bow ties. They smiled at Roxie.

'Waiting staff,' Ethan explained, leading her out of the back door and into the garden.

The scent of roses filled the air, heady and romantic, comforting and uplifting. More of the battery-operated candles ran across the paving stones and towards a large white marquee that had been erected on the lawn. Fairy lights twinkled out here too, draped around the edges of the marquee, around the fencing of the decking and across a DJ table. A man wearing a white linen suit and black flat cap waved to her from up there, so she waved back then music filled the air, a seventies disco tune that she'd loved as a girl.

As if summoned by the music, Fletcher appeared at the entrance to the marquee. He had Glenda in his arms and looked very handsome in a white shirt, sleeves rolled up to the elbows, and dark chinos, his salt and pepper hair swept back from his broad forehead, his face clean-shaven. His skin was tanned, his eyes bright as they held her captive.

He held out a hand and Roxie took it, then they entered the marquee to calls of 'Surprise!' and 'Happy Anniversary!'

Roxie scanned the room, seeing her mum and dad, Joanne, Finlay, Freda and more. People smiled at her from every corner of the marquee including waiting staff in their uniform of black trousers, white shirts and bow ties.

The music seemed to get louder as she stood there, the scent of flowers overpowering, faces of family and friends loomed towards her and she could barely catch her breath.

'Happy anniversary, Roxie,' Fletcher said, holding her hand tight, Glenda still supported by his other arm. 'We have something we want to say to you.'

Roxie looked at him, her handsome husband, the man she had loved and adored for so long. Her heart swelled in her chest and her throat constricted with emotion. She squeaked, 'I can't. I'm sorry.'

Then she snatched her hand away, turned and ran from the marquee, over the paving stones and into the house.

∽

Fletcher looked around him at the familiar faces, hurt and horror making him tremble. What had just happened? How had this all gone so wrong? Roxie hadn't even given him a chance to speak properly, to tell her what this was all about. And where had she gone?

He handed Glenda to Ethan who was waiting by the entrance, his brows knitted in confusion then shrugged before chasing after his wife.

Inside, the house was cool, the windows thrown open to let in the evening air. The cheering fragrance of flowers met him as he walked through the hallway, checked the lounge, then padded up the stairs. When Roxie had arrived, he'd been delighted, certain that this was what they needed, that she'd be happy and see that he loved her, had always been true to her, but instead, it had backfired and he was terrified that he'd lost her for good.

Her perfume, a delightful combination of tuberose and jasmine, led him to their bedroom where he found her perched on the end of their bed, her face pale, her eye make-up smudged, but even now she looked beautiful.

'Roxie,' he said as he knelt in front of her and took her hands. 'What is it? Did I do the wrong thing?'

She looked up and he was hit by the brilliance of her green eyes, by their pretty almond shape and by how much he wanted to be able to gaze into them for the rest of his life.

'No, Fletcher. What you've done… it's amazing. You're such a good man, so loving and caring… But… I just feel awful.'

'Why, angel?' He rubbed his thumbs over her fingers, pressed his lips to the smooth skin.

'Because I've doubted you... because I've let you down.'

'What? How?'

She sighed and closed her eyes, her dark lashes fluttered on her cheeks.

'I thought... that perhaps you were having an affair.' She opened her eyes.

'Never!' His face felt tight with strain. 'Why would I want anyone else when I have you?'

'I couldn't give you a family.'

'Roxie... that was never an issue. I didn't need anyone other than you.'

'But after the... after we... lost the twins...' She blinked hard and he reached out and wiped a tear from her cheek. 'I couldn't bear to try again.'

'But we did try, Roxie, we did. It just didn't work out for us.'

'It might have done, Fletcher, but I couldn't bear to go through it all again. Losing our two tiny babies was just too painful.'

'We said that if it happened, it happened. It didn't and I'll be honest, I struggled with it for years, worried that it was me and that I was failing you. It's why I tried so hard to give you everything else you needed, everything you wanted. But I couldn't give you what I thought you wanted most of all... a family.'

His heart was fractured, broken by sadness as he finally let the thoughts he always pushed away back in. It had taken them two years to conceive from when they had decided to try, and they'd been overjoyed to find out at the first scan that they were expecting twins. Then, the day after their eighth wedding anniversary, Roxie had started bleeding and an emergency scan had found no heartbeats. The twins would have been almost seventeen now, young adults with their own lives ahead of them. The doctor at the hospital had said they could try again, but to wait a while to grieve and allow Roxie's body to recover.

'It wasn't you, Fletcher. I… took measures to stop it happening again. I was only going to take the pill for a year or two, just to let myself heal emotionally, but the idea of going through something so terrible again grew and grew so I could barely breathe when I thought about it. I hoped I could make you happy just by being a loving wife, by making our home warm and comfortable, by being supportive. I thought it could be enough.'

Fletcher sighed long and deep. 'Roxie, are you telling me that you didn't want children?'

'I did, desperately. I longed to hold our child in my arms. But after the twins… I just couldn't imagine being pregnant again.'

'Why didn't you tell me?' His voice wavered and fear filled her gaze.

'I couldn't… I didn't know how. I thought you'd hate me.'

He sat back on his heels and gently released her hands then rubbed at his eyes. Roxie hadn't wanted children; he hadn't let her down. If only they'd talked about it and shared their true feelings. When they got married, they'd planned to have a large family, unaware that it could go wrong, confident in their youth and vitality, their fecundity. The miscarriage had been a harsh wake-up call, utterly heartbreaking and Roxie had clearly struggled with it even more than he had. It had been her body that had carried their children, her body that had been flooded with hormones then had to return to normal with no babies to hold in her arms. She had cried for weeks and then stopped, seeming to settle into a kind of calm, and he'd hoped she'd been healing, inside and out, that she'd be okay. He'd thrown himself into work as a distraction from the pain and vowed to provide for her, to do what he could to make her happy. The sense he'd had of failing her when they didn't conceive again had been horrid, so he'd done everything he could to make it up to her.

'I would never have hated you, Roxie. Children would have been a bonus, the icing on our cake, but it was you I wanted. Only you I've *ever* wanted. If you'd told me, I'd have understood. I was… I was terrified of going through it again, of seeing you go through it again, and every month my heart sat in my mouth when I wondered if you'd have news.' He ran a hand over the back of his neck, feeling the tension in his spine, wondering how he'd never realised how Roxie really felt. 'I knew that I'd spend nine months terrified if we conceived again. I'd have been terrified for the baby, or babies, but more so for you. I couldn't have coped with losing you, Roxie, and I always knew that was a risk.'

Tears were flowing down her cheeks now, creating white lines through her make-up, plopping onto her beautiful black dress and sitting on the material like liquid diamonds.

'You don't hate me?' Her voice was quiet, her eyes finally revealing exactly how she was feeling. All this time he hadn't known how badly she'd suffered.

'You've been protecting us both, haven't you? You knew it would break us if we had to endure another loss, so you ensured that there wasn't a risk of it happening.'

She nodded.

'You are incredible, far stronger than you will ever know.'

He leant forwards, wrapped his arms around her waist and buried his face in her neck. Fletcher was never letting go of Roxie ever again.

~

Roxie held her husband tight. His arms around her, and his understanding, was exactly what she had needed. Fletcher hadn't just accepted her confession, he had understood, and she suddenly felt free. She'd loved being pregnant with the twins, had looked forward to being a mum for so many reasons, but the miscarriage, the D and C afterwards (that cleared all trace of her babies away so she could never even see them), the infection that followed, the soreness in her breasts and the tears that wouldn't stop falling... they had all torn her apart and left her certain that she couldn't put herself or Fletcher through it again. She had worried that he'd regret marrying her, that he'd hate her for failing to give him a family, but she had never seen regret in his eyes or resentment stamped on his features. He had been loving, caring, true and kind. She hadn't wanted to give him up, to surrender their love and so she hadn't, because he had made her feel loved and adored, he hadn't seemed to have any regrets.

Fletcher released her and met her gaze.

'What made you think things had changed between us?'

'You worked such long hours, seemed to grow distant. It didn't happen overnight but crept up on us gradually, and I missed you.'

'I thought you'd become cold with me.'

'No. No. I just... I was trying to protect myself from the pain of losing you, which I thought I was. Then, when all that happened with Cynthia... I thought you'd finally had enough.'

'She's no one to me, Rox. There will never be anyone for me other than you. I was scared I was losing you.'

'Never.' She smiled but her throat ached with emotion.

'Promise?'

'I promise. And... are you sure you don't want a younger woman?'

'Why would I?'

'So you can have children now.'

'If I can't have children with you then I don't want them. You are all that matters to me. Knowing that I didn't let you down is... it's freeing, if that makes sense?'

'I'm sorry for that. I should have told you sooner.'

'Don't be. Please. I'm relieved. Liberated. All that matters is that I know now, and we're together.'

'I love you so much.'

'I love you. Also… I have some news that I was saving for tonight.'

She ran her gaze over his face, wondering what else they could share.

'I'm taking redundancy.'

'Redundancy? I had no idea that you were thinking of leaving work.'

'I'm fed up of the commute, of having my mind so busy all the time, of missing you. The company wants to restructure, and they asked a few months ago if anyone was interested in taking a package. At first, I didn't think I was, but it's very generous, more than most firms would offer, and along with my full pension, it will leave us very comfortable indeed.'

'Are you sure you're ready to leave? I can't imagine you home all day.'

He laughed. 'I can freelance here and there, offer my services as a consultant if I want to keep my toes in the water, but I'm done with long days and business lunches and all that malarkey. I want to focus on us, take a few holidays, and see some of the world.'

'I can't believe it!' Roxie's stomach somersaulted. 'This is wonderful.'

'I'm glad you think so.' He lifted her hands and kissed the palms slowly, sending shivers of delight up and down her spine. 'We can reconnect…' His voice turned husky, his eyes darkened. 'In more ways than one.'

'Sounds good to me.' She slid her arms around his neck.

'Have I told you how sexy you are in that dress?' He ran his hands up and down her sides, sending delicious sensations through her body.

'No... but tell me now.'

'Oh, I will.'

He cupped her chin, moved closer, then kissed her passionately, and all her worries melted away.

~

Later on, when they'd rejoined their guests, Lila handed Roxie a champagne flute and Fletcher led her around the marquee to speak to everyone. Roxie's entire body felt lighter, as if an extremely heavy weight had been lifted. She had shared everything with Fletcher and he had with her, and now there was nothing left to fear. He was taking redundancy too, they would be able to spend more time together, and that was a wonderful anniversary gift.

'I have one more surprise,' he said, as he held up a hand and Ethan tapped a spoon on a glass. It seemed that this had been planned too.

'Another?' she asked, gazing at him in wonder.

'Yes,' he whispered. 'Thank you so much for coming.' Fletcher smiled at their guests. 'We are so grateful that you came to share this evening with us. Now... where's Glenda?'

A bark alerted him to the small dog's whereabouts; she was sitting on Lila's knee.

'Glenda, come here.' Fletcher clapped his hands and the pug jumped down and ran towards him. He picked her up then turned to Roxie. 'There's something on her collar for you.'

Roxie peered at Glenda's collar then gasped, because there was a ribbon tied to it, and on that ribbon was a ring. She untied the ribbon and held up the rose gold band set with two diamonds and a large opal. 'It's so beautiful.'

'Just like you,' Fletcher said, then he knelt down and set Glenda on the floor.

'What are you doing?' She giggled.

'Hand me the ring.'

She did then he gently took her left hand.

'Roxie, my wife, my love, my best friend. Years ago, you agreed to be my wife. You made me the happiest man alive and we've shared many happy times, but also been there for each other through some very difficult ones. I believe that's what marriage is about… the good and the bad, the highs and the lows. To show you how much I love you still, and to celebrate that love, I'd like to ask you to marry me again. I'd like us to renew our vows. What do you think? Will you marry me again, Roxie?'

She looked around the marquee at their friends and family, at Glenda, who was sitting watching them as if she too was waiting to hear her answer then back at Fletcher.

'Of course, I'll marry you, Fletcher. I love you with all of my heart.'

He slid the ring onto her finger, and it sat perfectly above her other two rings.

Fletcher stood up and swept her into his arms, and as he kissed her, their guests cheered, Glenda barked, and Roxie's heart soared.

There would be many more happy summer days on Sunflower Street.

The End

DEAR READER,

Thank you so much for reading *SUMMER DAYS ON SUNFLOWER STREET*. I hope you enjoyed the story.

You can find me on Twitter **@authorRG,** on Facebook at **Rachel Griffiths Author** and on Instagram at **rachelgriffithsauthor** if you'd like to connect with me to find out more about my books and what I'll be working on next.

With love,
Rachel X

ABOUT THE AUTHOR

Rachel Griffiths is an author, wife, mother, Earl Grey tea drinker, gin enthusiast, dog walker and fan of the afternoon nap. She loves to read, write and spend time with her family.

ALSO BY RACHEL GRIFFITHS

CWTCH COVE SERIES

CHRISTMAS AT CWTCH COVE

WINTER WISHES AT CWTCH COVE

MISTLETOE KISSES AT CWTCH COVE

THE COTTAGE AT CWTCH COVE

THE CAFÉ AT CWTCH COVE

CAKE AND CONFETTI AT CWTCH COVE

A NEW ARRIVAL AT CWTCH COVE

THE COSY COTTAGE CAFÉ SERIES

SUMMER AT THE COSY COTTAGE CAFÉ

AUTUMN AT THE COSY COTTAGE CAFÉ

WINTER AT THE COSY COTTAGE CAFÉ

SPRING AT THE COSY COTTAGE CAFÉ

A WEDDING AT THE COSY COTTAGE CAFÉ

A YEAR AT THE COSY COTTAGE CAFÉ (THE COMPLETE SERIES)

THE LITTLE CORNISH GIFT SHOP SERIES

CHRISTMAS AT THE LITTLE CORNISH GIFT SHOP

SPRING AT THE LITTLE CORNISH GIFT SHOP

SUMMER AT THE LITTLE CORNISH GIFT SHOP

THE LITTLE CORNISH GIFT SHOP (THE COMPLETE SERIES)

SUNFLOWER STREET SERIES

SPRING SHOOTS ON SUNFLOWER STREET

SUMMER DAYS ON SUNFLOWER STREET

AUTUMN SPICE ON SUNFLOWER STREET

CHRISTMAS WISHES ON SUNFLOWER STREET

A WEDDING ON SUNFLOWER STREET

A NEW BABY ON SUNFLOWER STREET

NEW BEGINNINGS ON SUNFLOWER STREET

SNOWFLAKES AND CHRISTMAS CAKES ON SUNFLOWER STREET

A YEAR ON SUNFLOWER STREET (SUNFLOWER STREET BOOKS 1-4)

THE COSY COTTAGE ON SUNFLOWER STREET

SNOWED IN ON SUNFLOWER STREET

SPRINGTIME SURPRISES ON SUNFLOWER STREET

AUTUMN DREAMS ON SUNFLOWER STREET

A CHRISTMAS TO REMEMBER ON SUNFLOWER STREET

STANDALONE STORIES

CHRISTMAS AT THE LITTLE COTTAGE BY THE SEA

THE WEDDING

ACKNOWLEDGMENTS

Thanks go to:

My gorgeous family. I love you so much! XXX

My author and blogger friends, for your support, advice and encouragement.

Everyone who buys, reads and reviews this book.

Printed in Great Britain
by Amazon